LANDSCAPE LOVE

RIVER FORD

Fidem Press

Landscape Love

ISBN: 1722077298

ISBN-13: 978-1722077297

Cover Design by SelfPubBookCovers.com/RLSather

❀ Created with Vellum

To all the strong, feisty women out there who don't need a man but wouldn't mind a good one willing to hold her hand on her journey through life.

~River Ford

FEBRUARY

The woman in the hospital bed squeezed her eyes shut. Her gray hair fluffed around her head, the tiny wisps catching the air currents. Nate heard her labored breathing, the beeps of various machines, and the rhythmic hiss of the oxygen. His heart ached. Lilly Connor would have suffered through this alone if he hadn't been here.

"Stop scowling. I thought we cured you of that." Her voice was soft, but it still carried the sass he'd grown used to over the last two years.

"I promise to do better." He took her hand in his. Her skin was paper dry and loose over her knuckles. "How are you feeling?"

"Like it'll be over soon." She took a long time to blink.

"Don't say that."

"Eh, it's time, and I'll be glad to finally be with my Josiah again." She sighed and tried to sit up. Nate helped her shift the pillows until she was more comfortable. "There's only the one regret."

He nodded. He knew exactly to what she referred. All these years, and she'd never been able to heal the rift with her

1

only daughter, Abby. Because of that, she'd never met her grandchildren. Even so, she changed her will so one of them, a certain Lilliana Ramirez from Dallas, would inherit everything.

Previously, it had been slated to go to Mrs. Lilly's brother-in-law—Nate's boss, Brandon Connor. Nate couldn't care less about the little cottage or the clutter that filled it, and he knew his boss didn't want it either. But he didn't think the younger Lilly deserved anything from the sweet woman who'd adopted him as her own.

The granddaughter had never visited. Never called or written letters that he knew of. None of them had.

"Nathaniel, I said to stop." She scolded him again, and he tried to shift his thoughts. "I know you don't approve, but it's none of your business."

"Yes, ma'am."

"Now, I need your help." She waved him closer like she didn't want anyone to overhear. "I need you to exercise Gypsy until Lilly gets here. I don't trust no one else."

"You know I love Gyp as much as you." Nate thought of the mare Mrs. Lilly boarded at a ranch outside of town. The old lady, as he called the horse, was getting up in years but was as gentle as ever. He wondered what the younger Lilly would do with the horse.

"There's one more thing." Mrs. Lilly had a glint in her eyes. The kind that always meant trouble for him. "You'll have to teach my granddaughter how to ride. She may live in Texas, but I can't find any trace she's ever been around horses."

Nate cringed. "Mrs. Lilly, I don't think—"

She lifted her hands like she was going to wave them at him, but halfway up they dropped back to the bed. "No, listen. She'll be new here and won't know anyone. She's gonna need someone to help her out."

"Someone will step up." He swallowed a lump in his throat.

"I'm asking you to step up." Mrs. Lilly wilted into the pillows. The little color she had, faded. "Please, do it for me."

Nate squeezed the old woman's bony hand. She'd gone out of her way to make him feel welcome the last two years. To make him smile when he thought he never would again. She was the only one who knew why he'd left his home in Colorado.

The last thing he needed was to run into the prodigal granddaughter. But Mrs. Lilly had become a surrogate grandmother. The least he could do was honor her last wish.

"Okay."

"Good." She patted his hand. "One last thing. Forgive yourself and get on with your life. You're too young to mope around like this."

"I don't think—" he started.

"No, you think too much and don't feel. Your wife wouldn't have wanted that for you."

"Probably not." The familiar sadness proved he still felt more than he cared to.

"Then do us all a favor and start smiling."

"Yes, ma'am." He practiced one just for her. It felt unnatural, but after she was gone she wouldn't know if he never did it again.

∽

*L*illy Ramirez leaned forward, gripping the steering wheel with both hands. Her family dynamics had changed overnight, and her head was still spinning. She'd been at work when a lawyer found her and delivered a large envelope of papers.

Thank goodness her boss had been around to help her

3

deal with the shock of what they contained. Lilly never knew she had a grandmother living somewhere in Arkansas. Now she'd passed away, and it was too late to meet her.

After a yelling match about keeping secrets with Abby, her mom, Lilly had run home to her apartment and packed a bag. She tossed and turned in bed a few hours before leaving Dallas and heading for Eureka Springs, Arkansas.

She drove six hours straight, only stopping for gas and bathroom breaks. Now she was tired and cranky, on top of being emotionally raw.

The highway had given way to hilly, winding roads. To make matters worse, her GPS kept rerouting, and cars lined up behind her slow forward motion. If she couldn't find her grandma's house soon, she'd have to drive back to town and ask for directions. Lilly didn't feel like talking to anyone in her sensitive state.

Abby had made it clear she didn't want Lilly going to Eureka Springs. Her final warning still rang in her ears. "I'll never speak to you again if you go to that town. Not after the way they treated your father."

Even though she worried about the ultimatum, Lilly had to know more about her maternal grandma. She'd walked away, knowing Abby wasn't joking or tossing out idle threats. The fact that Abby had hidden her own mother's existence for all twenty-eight years of Lilly's life was proof of that.

A stray tear escaped and she swiped at it. Even in her anger, she couldn't deny the fear. What if her choice ended her relationship with her mother? It had been strained for years, evident by Lilly's refusal to call Abby mom.

She'd have to trust that Papi could bring her around.

"*Ayudame.*" She whispered a plea for help. Shaking her head, she tried to calm down. Lilly only slipped into Spanish when she was tired, frustrated, or angry. Or when she was visiting her papi's family in Mexico. Her thoughts turned back to the unknown grandmother.

Grandma Connor, don't let me lose her over this. Lilly had started the conversation with her grandma an hour into the trip. It helped calm her down. Lilly told her about her life and all her worries, then she asked questions, hoping the little house would hold the answers.

If she could ever find it.

A peace settled in her heart. She took a shaky breath and relaxed her grip on the steering wheel.

"Re-routing..." The monotone voice shattered the moment of calm.

"Arggg! That's it." Lilly slapped the console.

She found a gravel drive and pulled in to let the other cars pass. Then she turned back toward Eureka Springs. It was time to give in and ask for help.

Lilly pulled into a little gift shop on the edge of town. It looked like it sold rocks and broken glass. Outside stalls held what looked liked rock dust, pebbles, small stones, all the way up to large garden-sized specimens.

The short walk from the car to the door reminded her she hadn't driven far enough north for the summer. Arkansas was every bit as hot and humid as home, and it would only get hotter as summer matured.

The store was divided into sections, the first one cluttered with red and white sports trinkets and clothing, all of it printed with "Go Razorbacks" or some hog image. She passed into the main area that contained a little of everything else and walked straight to the register and the woman staring at her.

"Excuse me. I'm looking for County Road one-seventeen." Lilly noticed two dogs lounging on a huge pillow behind the counter. One small, one large. They didn't even spare her a glance, clearly used to strangers coming in and out of the store.

The woman continued to gape over the rims of her glasses for another second. "You must be Mrs. Lilly's grand-daughter."

Lilly narrowed her eyes. "Yes. How did you know?"

"Small town, and we've all been waiting to meet you." The woman smiled, walked around the counter, and pulled Lilly into a hug. "Mrs. Lilly talked about you all the time. I wish you could have met her."

It wasn't a hug between strangers. This woman squeezed her tight like she was holding something dear. It startled Lilly so much a lump rose in her throat, and the tears gathered again. She blinked them away and allowed herself to hug the other woman before pulling away.

"Me too. What's your name?"

"Sorry. I'm Florence DeWitt. You can call me Flo. Half the town's been watching and waiting for you since the funeral first week of March."

"What?" Lilly didn't know what to think. They'd had three and a half months to anticipate her arrival while she was oblivious to their existence. It felt weird to think people might recognize her when she wouldn't know anyone.

"Like I said, small town." Flo waved her hand in the air. "Word gets around, and by the time Mrs. Lilly's funeral was over, we all knew she'd left everything to you. Feel free to ask for any help you might need."

Lilly tried not to shudder. Did the town wonder why her and not Abby? Or one of her older siblings? That one thing had infuriated Abby the most when she learned the details of the will. Lilly pushed that train of thought away. "Right now, I just want to find the house and get some sleep. It's just been a crazy night and an even longer drive."

Flo looked at her with sympathy. "I'm sure it has. The

house isn't hard to find once you know what you're looking for." She pulled out a piece of paper and drew a map. She pointed to the lines as she talked. "Go back down sixty-two, past the Thorncrown Chapel, and over the bridge. Another half mile to a mile you'll get to the gas station, turn left there. One-seventeen is the first road to the left after that. Mrs. Lilly's is all the way at the end."

"Thanks. I know I passed that gas station several times already." She took the map and turned for the door.

"Lilly? I don't think there's any food at the house. I live right down the road." She pointed toward the wall opposite her. "I put my address on the map. We eat around seven."

Lilly noticed that lump again. Abby had been adamant no one would embrace her jet black hair and olive skin, but this woman was warm and welcoming. She already felt more at home here than in her parents' mini-mansion. She nodded at Flo, afraid to say anything, and hurried to her car.

Feeling much more hopeful, she made her way back down the road. Maybe this summer wouldn't be as bad as she thought. Her boss told her to take all the time she needed to go through her grandma's estate. She'd planned to be fast, but maybe she'd stick around longer. She could learn about this hidden side of the family. A summer without Abby breathing down her back to "get a real job," as she put it, would be nice too. Lilly might even figure out how to fight for her own dreams.

She turned at the gas station and this time she found the little dirt road easily. Even though she drove slowly, enjoying the canopy the trees made over the road, a trail of dust grew behind her. Despite that, the world was green everywhere she looked.

She passed a couple of houses before reaching a mailbox at the end with the name "Connor" on it. Lilly couldn't see the house, but a little field dotted with trees and wildflowers made its way over a gentle hill, hiding what lay beyond. There was plenty of room to plant flowers, maybe even set up a greenhouse or two.

"Don't be silly." She pushed the thought to the back of her mind, but that spark of hope doubled. If she owned all this land, her goals might be more achievable than she'd thought.

The house sat next to the edge of a wood, almost disappearing into the trees. There was a spot of dirt to park on and several overgrown flowerbeds, but it was the house that held her attention. The hardboard siding was a dull gray, with cream trim that had seen better and brighter days. River rock lined the front patio, and the porch rail was covered in ivy and flowers that should have been trellised but roamed free instead. An old rocking chair on the front porch looked like a good place to soak in the peace and quiet only nature could offer.

Even lonely and forgotten, it was the most beautiful thing she'd ever seen. Its slightly wild look was the complete opposite of her parents' manicured home. That endeared it to her even more.

The gardens contained bright spots of color peeking through the overgrown weeds, calling the plant lover in her to get her hands dirty.

Later.

She grabbed her cell phone and called her mom. It went straight to voicemail.

"Abby, I made it to Eureka Springs. Just wanted you to know. Call me." She paused, thinking of all the fights they'd had the last few years. "Love you."

She hit end and grabbed her purse. The screen door made a lovely sound when she opened it. Her hand shook as she lifted the key. It took two tries before she managed to get the door unlocked.

Inside was dark. The thick smell of a closed-up house,

mingled with old furniture and years of greasy southern cooking, greeted her. Lilly recognized it for what it was—the scent of a woman she'd never know.

Lilly flipped the light switch to reveal a cozy place filled with vintage furniture, lots of doilies, and other knick-knacks. Exhaustion set in. She moved through the house, opening the windows to let the stuffiness out, before finding her grandma's bed and falling into it. Even the heat didn't bother her as she succumbed to the much-needed sleep.

TUESDAY

*N*ate mentally shook a fist at Mrs. Lilly in heaven. How she messed with his life from up there was beyond him. And yet she'd been at it for the last two months. She'd sent little reminders all around town about the life he'd run away from. He'd saved a stray dog after it got hit by a car, reminding him how much he'd loved being a veterinarian. The influx of tourists reminded him he used to be social, and then there was Jaya and Aiden. That one hurt the most.

Connor Landscaping had been hired to help build a memorial to Aiden after he died in a car accident, and Mr. Connor asked Nate to oversee the project. Nate had struggled to keep it together and almost quit several times. Watching Jaya deal with her childhood sweetheart's death hit too close to home.

He considered leaving town but figured Mrs. Lilly's ghost would follow him around until he felt guilty enough to come back and do what he'd promised. That lovable, geriatric meddler. She told him before passing she would set him on the straight and narrow. He felt silly for laughing at her now.

Who knew an old woman could be so determined from beyond the grave?

His happy irritation faded quickly under the sadness. If Mrs. Lilly could manipulate him from heaven, why hadn't his wife tried to communicate with him?

Don't think about it.

He refocused on the task at hand. The faster he got this over with, the better. Flo had called around one to inform him the granddaughter had arrived in town. She called again at eight.

"She's out there all alone with no food, Nate. Mrs. Lilly would be ashamed of us if we didn't take her something."

"How do you know she didn't go out?"

"Roberta said her car is still parked in the drive."

"Why didn't Roberta take her something?" Roberta lived on the same dirt road as Mrs. Lilly.

"Nate, stop wasting time and take her some food."

"Why can't she go to the store like everyone else?" He wanted no part of welcoming the new Lilly to town.

"I'm sure she will, but she looked so tired and alone. She almost broke down in tears when I hugged her. I don't think that poor child knows which way is up or down right now."

"I don't see how that's any of my concern."

"Nathaniel Pierce, you promised you'd help Mrs. Lilly's granddaughter." Flo used that tone every mother knew. The one that slapped you into place without leaving a visible mark.

"How do you know about that?"

"Mrs. Lilly told everyone in town to call you if we saw her granddaughter in need."

Nate groaned.

He'd get phone calls about the new Lilly until she left town. In the end, he decided it would be better to help her on her way quickly. Maybe then Mrs. Lilly's ghost would let him be. She couldn't expect him to take care of the granddaughter once she left Eureka Springs.

But that didn't mean he had to be happy about it. Nate grabbed take-out from his favorite restaurant, ordering one of the spiciest burgers on the menu just to soothe his rage, and headed out of town. His stomach churned with anger the whole time. It kicked up when he turned his pickup down the dirt road leading to Mrs. Lilly's. He'd have to play nice even though he didn't think much of the estranged family. Who knew what Abby had told her kids about the older woman he'd grown to respect. The fact they took so long to send someone to check out the old house didn't help.

The sun sank low in the sky. It backlit the cottage, giving it a warm friendly glow. He just wished Mrs. Lilly was sitting in the rocker on the front porch. With a sigh, he parked under the big oak tree and grabbed the Sparky's takeout bag.

All the windows were up, a light breeze making the curtains flutter. The front door was open, with just the screen door blocking his entry. For a moment, he almost forgot to knock. He'd always walked in before.

Nate pounded the door with a heavy hand and was rewarded with a yelp and a thump that sounded like something falling to the floor. Shortly after, a head popped around the corner of Mrs. Lilly's bedroom. A woman with delicate bone structure, perfect olive skin, and a head of straight, silky black hair hanging free around her face stared back at him. Her sleepy eyes were dark and expressive.

She approached the door but didn't open it. The woman was taller than her grandmother, but not by much. Her head would nestle nicely on his shoulder or in the crook of his neck.

Where did that thought come from?

He pushed it away but took in every detail of the woman before him. His gaze moved from her loose T-shirt to the pair of cut-off jeans. Her legs were smooth and sculpted all the way down to her bare feet and toes that sported bright orange nail paint. His body responded to the woman, in spite of his determination not to like anything about her.

Down boy. This was definitely not what he expected. *Just because she's gorgeous doesn't mean she's nice.*

Young Lilly, as he'd been calling her in his mind, peered up at him. Little wisps of hair clung to her neck, damp with perspiration.

"Can I help you?"

"I'm Nate Pierce. Mrs. Lilly left the town instructions to call me if you needed anything." He held up the bag of take-out. "Mrs. DeWitt called and said you needed dinner."

"Florence?" A little crinkle appeared between her brows. "Oh! I forgot to go to her house. I'll have to apologize tomorrow. Please, come in." She opened the door and waved him in.

Nate couldn't believe she remembered Flo's name. The heartless woman he'd envisioned over the last year wouldn't have. She certainly wouldn't look disappointed at forgetting dinner either.

He stepped inside. Everything looked the same as the last time he'd stopped by to water the plants. The slightly musty smell was gone, thanks to the open windows. It helped him relax even though it was unbearably warm.

"You know you can turn on the air." He pointed to the window unit.

"I fell asleep before I got that far." She shrugged her shoulders before walking over to switch it on. "Did you know my grandma?"

Sleeping in the day? Definitely pampered. "Hungry?"

"Yes." She smiled, and all his annoyance went up in smoke. Then she turned and practically danced her way to the kitchen.

"Um, yeah." He had to drag his eyes away from her swaying backside to remember what she'd asked him. "I took care of her yard. Mowed it, helped weed and plant, that kind of thing." Concentrating on the back of her head, he walked until he could set the bag on the small table. "I didn't know what you'd like, so I got my favorite." His gut gave a rebellious twist of guilt. He didn't mention that his favorite burger was spicy enough to bring a lesser man to tears.

"This wasn't necessary, but thank you." She pulled out two plates and set them on the table.

He had a sudden desire to grab that blasted bag and run. "I'm not eating."

"Oh, okay." She ducked her head, letting her hair sway forward to hide her face. Lilly turned and put one of the plates away. "Do you mind if I eat? I'm hungrier than I thought, and it smells wonderful."

"Sure." Nate reached in and reluctantly pulled out the Diablo burger. It wasn't the spiciest thing on the menu, but it rated three out of five flames. At the time he wanted to see her struggle with the heat. Now that he'd met her, he was having second thoughts. "It's a bit spicy."

"I love spicy food." She took the container from his hands, opened it, and took a huge bite of the messy burger before he could stop her.

Lilly chewed slowly, her eyes closed. A drop of chipotle sat on the edge of her mouth. Before he could say anything, her tongue darted out and licked it up. Nate had never thought watching someone eat was sexy, but he'd just been converted.

"*Maravilloso*." She looked at the bag. "Sparky's, huh? Do they have anything spicier?"

I could give you something spicier.

Nate almost jumped out of his seat at the thoughts running through his head. He hadn't been so turned on since

14

his wife died. He struggled to remind himself he didn't like this woman, but all he could do was wonder what else she could do with those lips.

Time to run. He stood. "Uh, yeah. I'll leave you to it."

"Wait." Lilly stood, resting a hand on his arm. "Please, I never got to meet my grandma. Since you knew her, I was hoping you'd tell me about her."

"What?" The scowl on his brow was more confusion than anger. Her touch had his whole arm electrified and waiting for her to do more. He swallowed. "I mean, you really want to know about her?"

"Well, yeah. I didn't know she existed until yesterday." Lilly stepped back and played with a napkin from the table.

"Yesterday? But she died over four months ago."

She shrugged, and when she looked up, her eyes were shiny. "The lawyer said it took awhile to clear all the paperwork."

"Aw, hell." The guilt cooled his heated body like a bucket of ice. Nate collapsed in the chair.

"What?" She leaned against the table, one eyebrow raised.

"Sorry. I, um." He scratched the stubble on his chin. "I thought you just didn't care enough to get here sooner."

"You thought I didn't care?" Her brows scrunched again, then her eyes dropped to the food in her hand before shooting back to him. She lifted the burger slightly with a questioning look on her face.

"Aw, hell." He pushed back from the table and headed for the door.

The sound of her bare feet slapping against the wood floor followed. Nate turned and braced himself for what he knew he deserved.

"You couldn't have known I like spicy foods." She waved the sandwich at him. "What was this?"

"If it makes any difference, I felt guilty about it as soon as I got here." He stepped back.

"And yet you gave it to me." She charged forward and shoved the burger into his chest, smearing cheese and sauce all over him with a twist of her wrist. "I'll get my own dinner from now on."

Nate caught the ruined meal before it fell to the ground, grateful he hadn't worn his favorite shirt. "But you liked it."

The fire in her eyes scorched his insides with the stream of angry words. "*Porque los hombres tienen que ser tan idiotas?*"

"What?" He retreated another step.

"What did I ever do to you?" She followed.

There wasn't a simple answer to that, and he didn't feel like explaining his relationship with the late Mrs. Lilly. That old broad still had him tied in knots. He could almost hear her laughing in heaven about the predicament he'd put himself in.

"Nothing. You've done nothing." He shook his head.

"Good to know I'm not the crazy one here." She grabbed him by the elbow and pinched.

"What are you doing?"

Lilly proceeded to push and shove him toward the door. "Get out, and take your stupid burger with you."

He almost laughed at such a petite woman trying to manhandle him, but the glare and determined set of her mouth kept him in check. Before he could figure out what to do or say, Nate found himself on the front porch holding the remains of the hamburger.

"Consider your job done." Lilly slammed the door.

He heard it click as the lock fell into place.

"Well, I'll be..." The whole experience had him spinning, and the worst part was knowing another busybody would call him. He'd end up right back here having to face the fire-cracker beauty.

For a moment he looked forward to that before reality set in.

Nate tossed the food away from the house. *Let the animals have it, and if anyone dares call, I'll tell them no.*

~

*L*illy sagged against the door. She was tired of people judging her when they knew nothing about her. At least it was understandable with strangers, but this guy took it too far. The fact she'd liked the look of him made her angrier. He'd started off nice enough, even with his gruff attitude.

Her stomach growled.

"And the burger was really good." She sighed and headed for the kitchen to scrounge for something to eat. The take-out bag still sat on the table. "Please let there be fries."

She peeked inside and was delighted to see some in the bottom, then realized they were the ones left behind from a missing container.

"He ate my fries!" She scooped up the four left in the bag and ate them while looking through the cabinets. "He's really going to get a piece of my mind if I see him again."

It looked like someone had cleared out all the perishables. There was no bread or crackers, just canned vegetables, chili, beans, and an unopened jar of salsa. That last item made her smile. Her grandma liked salsa.

She grabbed a can of chili and the salsa. Next, she found the pantry. Luckily there was some flour and cooking oil inside. "It'll do."

She kept looking until she found a small pot to warm the chili, then cleaned off a section of countertop to make tortillas.

Lilly didn't think of herself as overly Spanish. She was

17

American through and through. She spoke Spanish because her papi and his family spoke it. She did like spicy foods. However, she would have preferred that burger to the lame homemade tortillas with canned chili. Jarred salsa probably wouldn't make it any better.

She mixed the flour with some salt, water, and a tiny bit of oil. After rolling them out, she fried them in a dry pan using salt to keep them from sticking. She spread the chili in the warm tortilla and topped it with some of the salsa.

It was passable, just as she feared. What she wouldn't give for some cheese, lettuce, fresh tomatoes, and avocados.

Lilly's mind drifted to Nate Pierce. Mercy, he'd been nice to look at. His dark hair had been all messed up as if he'd tried to fix hat hair. She could see the line in the back when he turned to leave.

And those eyes! *Azul* fit much better than plain old blue. Yeah, his eyes needed to be described with a romance language. She rolled around the Latin word caeruleum, but it felt too formal. Nate's eyes were sinfully hot, nowhere near stuffy enough for a dead language like Latin.

"So much wasted information in my mind." She shook her head in disgust. Who knew Latin?

She did.

How many years had she wasted learning stuff her mother thought would be worthwhile? Latin was one of those things. When her siblings found interests her mom approved of, Abby stopped nagging them to do better. Lilly was the only one she still badgered and complained about.

Lilly pulled out her phone. No texts or missed calls from Abby. "At least she won't bug me if she's not talking to me."

She sighed and dumped the rest of her dinner in the trash.

WEDNESDAY MORNING

"Good morning, Florence." Lilly smiled at the lady behind the counter.

"Seriously, call me Flo." It only took a moment for her to zip around and give Lilly a hug. "How are you this morning?"

"Pretty good. I'm sorry I forgot to come to dinner. I fell asleep and didn't wake up until Nate knocked on the door."

"Oh, I'm sorry. I hope he brought you something good to make up for waking you."

"Um, yeah." Lilly shrugged.

"What did he bring? Nate keeps to himself and it's been hard for anyone to get to know him. Mrs. Lilly knew him better than anyone. She seemed to think him a good guy, but he doesn't talk much." Florence unpacked a box of t-shirts, folding and then placing them on a shelf while they talked.

"He, um, brought me a burger from Sparky's." Lilly felt slightly embarrassed about her part in the burger incident. She shouldn't have thrown it at him.

"They have some great stuff. Did you get chili cheese fries? Those are my favorite." She collapsed the box and set it behind the register. The dogs were sleeping, same as the day before. "What are your plans for today?"

Lilly sighed with relief. "I'm going grocery shopping, and then I'll start digging through the boxes upstairs. I'd also like to find people to talk to about Mrs. Lilly, you know, get to know more about her."

"There'll be plenty of people willing to talk. In fact, I bet they'll start knocking on your door as soon as word gets out you're settled in."

"I look forward to that. Where can I shop for food?"

"Hart's. Just follow the road and you'll see it off to the left after a while."

"Hart's, got it. Well, I'd better get going. Thanks again for all your help yesterday." Lilly turned to the door, then paused. "By the way, what's with all the wart hogs?"

Flo's eyes rounded, then she bent over laughing. "Honey, don't let anyone else hear you calling them that. Those are razorbacks. Much fiercer. It's the University of Arkansas mascot."

Lilly blushed. "Okay, sorry."

"Don't worry about it, dear. Just giving you a heads-up. People love their team around here." Flo's good-natured laugh followed her out the door.

The grocery store was easy to find, even if it did sit back from the road. Lilly pushed her cart up and down every aisle, not sure what she felt like buying. Eventually, she drifted to the TV dinners. It wasn't that she couldn't cook; she simply didn't want to use the oven and add to the heat in the house unless absolutely necessary. Plus, she'd be busy sorting through all of Mrs. Lilly's belongings.

She was trying to remember if there'd been a microwave in the kitchen when movement off to the side caught her attention. She turned to see Nate Pierce staring at her. He was wearing jeans, a dark gray T-shirt, and a ball cap that read "Connor Landscaping." He had a funny look on his face that almost hinted of fear. It would have been comical if not for the bag of frozen french fries in his hands.

She pointed at them. "That reminds me."

"Of what?" He scowled.

"You ate my fries."

Nate rubbed the back of his neck. "I, um."

He looked so uncomfortable Lilly took pity on him. She wasn't angry anyway. Luckily, her mother hadn't passed down the grudge-keeping trait.

"Forget it." She waved him off and went back to studying the frozen foods. *Forgiveness is one thing, but getting cozy is out of the question. Right?*

"Miss Ramirez?" Nate stepped closer.

She glanced at him again. He really was eye-candy yummy. Those wide shoulders, flat abs. Lilly had to gulp down a sigh. Maybe they could be friends as long as she didn't let him distract her from the real reason she was in town. "Oh, please. Call me Lilly."

"Can we start over?"

"I don't know. Are you always a jerk?" She couldn't help it and smiled when she asked.

"Sadly, yes." He shrugged, but the small grin that tilted his lips almost took her breath away. That smile changed Nate from country cute to dangerously good looking.

Lilly examined the square tiles on the floor. "At least you're honest about it."

He chuckled, drawing her gaze back to him. It was a nice sound to go with a gorgeous face.

Stay focused. "Then tell me, why did you try to do me in with a burger? Which, I might add, was shamefully wasted with my outburst. Sorry about that."

"You don't want to know." He shook his head.

"Sure I do."

He rubbed his chin. "All right. First, it really is my favorite burger. Second, I knew Mrs. Lilly for almost two years. During that time, none of your family ever came to visit. Not a letter, postcard, or phone call as far as I could tell." Nate paused, but his gaze grew more intense as he looked into her eyes. "Your grandmother meant a lot to me, but I'm not family. One of you should have been with her at the end. Not me."

Slapping her would've hurt less. Lilly covered her heart with her hand. "But I didn't know about her."

The thought of her grandma suffering alone weighed Lilly down. She leaned against the cart for support. Nate had been there. Her grandmother hadn't been completely alone.

"I'm glad she had you." Lilly glanced at her empty basket. "I'd better get back to shopping. At this rate, I'll never get lunch."

"Lunch." Nate looked at the watch on his wrist. "I owe you a meal. How about I treat you to Sparky's and you can pick your own burger this time?"

A little thrill coursed through her. Lunch with Nate sounded deliciously dangerous. Her stomach growled.

"I'll take that as a yes?" His brows tilted up.

Lilly laughed. "Guess so. Do I get fries this time?"

"Of course."

Her stomach rumbled again. "How far is this restaurant? I may shop after we eat."

"It's within walking distance."

Lilly grabbed her purse and left the cart in the aisle. "Let's go, then."

She heard Nate toss the frozen fries back into the freezer before following her. They stepped into the summer heat, and Lilly pulled big red sunglasses from her bag.

"Okay, Hollywood. Up the parking lot and to the left."

"Hollywood, huh? Is that the best you've got?" She tried

not to smile since he probably hadn't meant it as a compliment.

"Yep. Come on." Nate led her the short walk to Sparky's.

She stared at the restaurant, not understanding what she was looking at. It looked like two buildings smooshed together. One side had red trim, the other green.

Nate opened the door for her. "You coming?"

"Yeah."

The inside was just as strange as the outside, but somehow it felt welcoming. She wasn't sure how to label the place. Cafe, diner, someone's idea gone horribly wrong? There was a small dining area on one side for private groups, the register and some souvenirs in the middle, then down a step to a 50s diner type area. Nate turned toward the diner.

Lilly felt all eyes turn toward them. She tried hard to ignore them, telling herself it was because everyone knew she was new to town and not because she looked different from them. Darn Abby for planting the idea they wouldn't accept her because of her heritage.

"Hey, Nate." A teenage girl walked over and grinned at him. "Is this the new Lilly?"

Nate's hand rested on Lilly's lower back, sending a slow burn radiating through the rest of her. He nudged her forward. "Yeah, I had an accident with her burger, so I thought I'd bring her to the source."

"We're glad you're here. Mrs. Lilly talked about you all the time." The girl reached over and grabbed two menus and some silverware.

"She did?" Lilly asked.

The girl winked at her. "Sure did. It was her dream to get you here."

"Oh." All the confusion was back. "I wish she'd invited me sooner. And in a different way."

"I'm Belinda." The girl balanced her load in one arm and

squeezed Lilly's hand. "Mrs. Lilly was a real character. She had her own way of doing things, but Mom says we can't change people or their choices, just love and accept them anyway. That's what the Lord would have us do."

Lilly's heart thumped irregularly in her chest. So far everyone had been so nice. They smiled and tried to comfort her, and now this girl talked about love and acceptance. This town was definitely *not* like her mom had led her to believe.

"Thank you for that," she mumbled, not sure what else to say.

"Any free tables?" Nate interjected.

Lilly had almost forgotten he was there. The heat from his hand had turned to one of comfort, and she smiled up at him in thanks.

"You okay with outside?" Belinda looked back and forth between them.

"That's fine." Nate nodded.

The waitress led them to another area decorated completely different from the first two. This one had more of a ranch feel, with wood beams and a tin roof. Fans moved the air around, and the fabric sides had been rolled up all along the walls for breeze optimization. It was warm, but not unpleasant. Strings of lights hung from the rafters and music filled the air. Lilly found her feet tapping to its rhythm after she slid into the booth.

"The specials are on the board over there." Belinda pointed to a whiteboard. "What do you want to drink?"

"I'll have a root beer." Nate played with the napkin holder in the middle of the table.

"Just water for me," Lilly answered when Belinda turned her way.

"Okay, I'll be back for your order in a minute."

She hurried away, and Lilly focused on the menu in front

of her. Everything looked good. She barely made it past chips and guacamole before Belinda returned with their drinks.

"Here you go. Are you ready?"

"What did you order before?" Lilly finally made eye contact with the man sitting across from her. His blue eyes looked stormy gray today.

"Diablo burger." He ducked his head when Belinda punched his shoulder.

"You took her a Diablo burger? You really are an idiot." She shook her head.

"I believe I called him an idiot too." Lilly laughed. "Lucky for him I like spicy stuff and am the forgiving type. I'll have another Diablo burger, and Flo said I had to get chili cheese fries."

"Good choice." Belinda scribbled something on her pad of paper.

"I'll have the same." Nate locked gazes with Lilly.

The way he looked at her sent a little shiver down her spine. It felt like he wanted to eat her. If only she didn't wish he'd try.

"Be back soon." Belinda hurried away again.

Lilly grabbed her drink and gulped half of it down. She needed to cool off.

"Thirsty?" His eyes twinkled.

Lord help her if he knew what she was thinking! Lilly swallowed. She needed to take charge of the conversation, steer it away from the uncharacteristic urges threatening to derail her.

"So, how did you meet my grandma?"

"I mowed her field and delivered plants. She would work in her garden while I did the field, then she'd invite me in for lemonade and apple pie."

She tried to imagine the scene. "I don't even know what she looked like."

"I'm sure there are pictures somewhere. I caught her looking at one of her husband once."

"Maybe I'll find it as I go through everything." Lilly thought of the boxes of stuff in the upstairs rooms. It seemed her grandma was a bit of a hoarder. Although it would make it easier to get to know her, it would be a lot of work. "She has a lot of stuff."

Nate nodded. "So, how did you find out about her?"

Lilly stacked the salt and pepper shakers on top of the napkin holder. How much did she want to share? In the end, she figured everyone would ask her the same question. Maybe if she told him, Nate could tell everyone else and she wouldn't have to keep repeating it.

"I was at work, and a lawyer came looking for me."

"Huh. Do you like where you work?" Nate's gaze never strayed from her face.

It made her feel even more self-conscious, but not necessarily in a bad way. "Yeah, I work in a flower shop, but I'd rather run my own greenhouse as a supplier." Lilly knocked the shakers off the tower she'd made. "Sorry, I don't usually tell people that."

"Why not?" Nate helped her pick them up.

"Habit, I guess. Abby doesn't think that's a worthwhile life goal."

"Why not, and why do you call your mom Abby?"

Lilly's face heated again. "It's a hangover from my senior year of high school. She insists on calling me Lilliana, which I hate, so I started calling her Abby. Which she hates. Childish, I know, but oddly satisfying too."

"And why doesn't she think growing flowers is a good business choice?"

"Don't know." Lilly stared at the tablecloth. She loved everything about growing flowers and plants. It was the only place she felt at peace, but even that had been tainted. How

26

many times had she been told to quit wasting time? That she'd never amount to anything if she didn't try harder?

"Better throw some salt over your shoulder to ward off bad luck," Nate joked.

"Too late for that." Lilly appreciated his attempt to lighten the mood.

"Huh?" Nate's eyes softened for half a second.

She tried to wave him away. "Never mind."

"Come on, you can't tease me like that."

"If I tell you, you have to tell me something personal in return."

"Okay." He squirmed in his seat. "What do you want to know?"

"I think I'll hold my question until I think of something really good to ask."

"Great, I look forward to it." His expression screamed the opposite.

Lilly laughed. "I bet you do."

"So, your bad luck?"

"My life's been pretty good, really. A little friction with Abby, but I've recently learned that could have been worse. I have four siblings I adore, even if they are overachievers. Abby wants me to be more like them."

He leaned back in the booth. "Why does your mom want you to be more like your siblings?"

"Well, they're all doing things she thinks are worthwhile. We've got an ER doctor, a fundraising genius for a children's home, an Air Force engineer, and a professional ballet dancer."

"Sounds like she thinks your greenhouses are too ordinary. Maybe she thinks you're too talented for that?"

"She doesn't know what my talents are. But I doubt she'll ever speak to me again. By coming here, I've sided with Lilly Connor on what happened years ago."

Belinda arrived with their food. It all looked and smelled wonderful. Lilly reached for a fry.

"Careful, they're straight from the fryer," Belinda warned her. "I'll bring some more water."

"Thanks." Lilly watched her hurry off again, stopping to check on three other tables on her way to the back. When Lilly refocused on Nate, he was watching her, not touching his food. "What?"

"You came anyway." It wasn't really a question.

Lilly struggled to keep the rising panic at bay. Instead, she focused on what her father had promised before she left for Eureka Springs.

"Papi, that's my dad, always said, '*La familia es lo mas valioso en la vida.*' That means family is the most important thing in the world. He encouraged me to come and promised to talk with Abby. I just hope she'll forgive me for disobeying her this time."

Lilly wasn't hungry anymore. She stared at the burger, waiting for the knot in her throat to relax. Her family was important, but she was being forced to choose one side over the other.

~

*L*illy looked terrified, pushing her food around the plate. More like a lost child than that vibrant, fiery woman he'd seen at the house the night before.

"Do you think family is the most important?" he asked.

Lilly nodded. "They make us who we are. Papi said he never agreed with mama about keeping Grandma Connor a secret, but he honored Abby's wishes. He tried to get Abby to speak with her mom for years after they married."

She stopped speaking and swallowed a few times. She looked at the wall, the tables across the room, everywhere but him. Lilly had proof her mom could hold a grudge, and yet she'd come anyway.

"Talk it out." He saw her hands fist and unfist beside her plate.

"Okay. My mother was really angry the other night. Even though she's hard on me, I've always known she loves me. But." She took a deep breath. "The last time I was with her, I didn't feel that."

She paused, and Nate urged, "Keep going. I promise I'm done judging."

Lilly nodded and leaned forward. "I've never seen her so worked up. She said her mom had forbidden her to date Papi because he was Hispanic. That's why they ran away."

"I knew that much. Your grandma felt bad about it. She tried to apologize many times over the years."

"That's what Papi said. He forgave her a long time ago. He told me he sent pictures of all of us when we were born." Lilly looked directly at him, a little of the fire back in her eyes. "I told you why I call mom Abby. The other night my dad told me why she insisted on always calling me Lilliana."

"Why?"

"Right before I was born, Papi tried to get Abby to reconcile again. When she wouldn't, he listed my name on the birth certificate as Lillian instead of Selena. Abby was furious. Papi insisted it stay but compromised enough to change it to Lilliana. He said he didn't push her after that because Abby almost left him. Funny how one letter helped."

"So you were named after your grandma."

"Yeah, I still can't believe it." She laughed softly and shook her head.

Nate had a hundred questions, but mostly he wanted to know how she hadn't known about her grandma. It just didn't seem possible.

"Didn't you ever ask about your mother's family?"

"Sure. We spent lots of time with my *abuelos* Ramirez. They lived close when we were little, and once they moved back to Mexico, we traveled down every summer. Abby said her whole family was dead. She never spoke of them, and when I asked for pictures, she yelled at me for worrying about dead people more than my chemistry grade. Looking back, that was a pretty ridiculous fight."

"You didn't look them up online? Just out of curiosity?"

Lilly shrugged. "I never thought my mom would lie about something like that."

She had a good excuse for not being at Mrs. Lilly's hospital bed. What was his excuse for not being with his family now?

Guilt settled around his heart, but he shoved it away. He needed to focus on something other than what he'd left behind. Other than what he'd run away from.

Instead, he stoked the anger he'd been living with for months. Lilly hadn't even cared to find their obituaries or anything. "I would have looked them up."

She squared her shoulders. "I thought you were done judging? I was a teenager. I believed my mom, who, by the way, never told me their names. Trust me, Abby can redirect like nobody's business. It was easier to let it go."

"If you really thought the family was so important, you would have tried harder."

"Why? Abby said they were dead. Why would I keep looking?" Lilly's face flushed. Her eyes lit up again with that fire.

"Forget it. You're too stubborn to admit you didn't try."

"I just told you I didn't try. What is your problem?" Her shoulders tensed and her expression hardened.

"Nothing." He leaned back, realizing too late he was picking a fight with her to make himself feel better. He tried to smooth things over. "Maybe you didn't know how to

30

search for the information. All you had to do was search for your mom's birth certificate."

The color drained from her face. Her mouth moved a few times before she managed to speak. "I'd better get back to work."

Nate waved Belinda over. "Can I get the bill?"

"And a to-go box." Lilly reached into her purse and tossed a ten on the table. "That should pay for my food. If not, well, you owed me."

Nate pushed the money back to her. "I said I'd cover it."

"Take the stupid money." She ground the words out between clenched teeth.

"No. Lunch is on me."

"Try to give that to me again and it will be." She glared at him, looked pointedly at his chili fries, then took the box from Belinda, who'd appeared again. "Thanks."

Nate watched her put the uneaten food into the box. She looked half angry, half wilted. His stomach churned. He'd done it again. Made her mad and hurt her with his stupidity. It was probably for the best they didn't get too close, but darn if it didn't make him feel bad.

"I should give you my number in case you need anything. The folks in town will just call me anyway." Nate pulled a business card from his wallet. "Might as well cut out the middleman."

"No thanks." She slid from the booth and hurried away, ponytail swinging.

She looked good from behind. Nate sighed and pocketed her ten. He'd find some way to give it back to her.

"You've already run her off?" Belinda stood beside him, hands on hips.

Mouthy teenagers. "Don't you have tables to clean?"

"Look, you've always been nice to me, but it only took you twenty minutes to send her fleeing out the door. You've got to work on your personal skills if you're ever going to get another date."

Nate signed the credit card slip and stood. "It wasn't a date, and she has things to do."

"Whatever. You guys started off with the tension of two freshmen with only five minutes in the janitor's closet. Seriously, it was sizzling. You'd be stupid to let her get away."

"Well, we're not in high school and there's more to life than attraction."

"So you admit you've got the hots for her?" Belinda grinned at him.

"Belinda, stay out of everyone's business." Nate headed for the door, trying his best to ignore the laughter behind him.

WEDNESDAY NIGHT

$\mathcal{L}$illy stretched, twisted, and flexed as much of her body as she could. She'd been sitting in one of the upstairs bedrooms for hours going through boxes. The stuff had been men's clothing and tools, but there was an odd box of cigars.

She took her time, trying to imagine what her grandfather might have been like. Most of his clothes were everyday work stuff, but he had two suits that must have been nice in their time. The wide ugly ties made her laugh. Everything looked like it had been boxed up for a long time, and they smelled of the mothballs they'd been packed in.

The pleasant morning breeze died with the increasing heat of the day. Even though the trees sheltered the little house from the direct glare of the sun, Lilly wished for central air. There were window units downstairs, but not upstairs. The temperature slowly moved from toasty to sweltering.

"One more box, then I'll take a break." She glanced around until she spotted a smaller one. Running a pocket knife across the tape, she opened it up. Inside were all kinds of papers. "Jackpot!"

Lilly glanced through them quickly before taking the entire box downstairs. This was what she'd hoped to find—birth and death certificates, high school diploma, enlistment papers, newspaper clippings, and other things that would help her put together the life her grandparents had lived.

The heat level dropped a good ten degrees as she descended the stairs. She sighed with relief , then cranked up the AC in the front parlor. She sat the box on the coffee table and went to the kitchen to get another glass of water from the fridge. The otherwise-empty appliance reminded her she still needed to go shopping before the end of the day.

She'd been so upset after leaving Sparky's that she hadn't bothered going back into the store. Instead, she'd come home and ripped weeds from the flower beds.

Eventually, she realized Nate couldn't know his words poked at her insecurities. She'd never considered finding her grandparents by looking at her mom's birth certificate. That would have been so simple, but she didn't think of it.

Once she'd calmed down, she ate the cold burger and fries before tackling the stuff upstairs. The food was good, but she hoped to eat a warm burger one of these days. Until then, she'd have to make another trip into town for supplies.

"Papers first." She wandered back to the couch. "I'll put them in chronological order."

She spread them over the surface of the table and sofa, making piles for the different decades of her grandfather's life. There was a folder of short stories he'd written in high school she couldn't wait to read. But she added them to a pile, determined to sort the entire box first.

There wasn't much after his birth certificate until he reached high school. Then there were awards for 4-H speaking and poetry, his diploma, and a few letters from her

grandma. There were more letters after the enlistment docu-
ments. Some postmarks were faded, but Lilly put them in
order as best she could. She wished she had the letters her
grandpa had sent in return. Maybe she'd find them in
another box somewhere.

After the war, there was a marriage certificate and
yellowed newspaper announcement. The black and white
photo showed a handsome man in uniform and a bright-
eyed girl. Her hair wasn't dark, but it wasn't light either.
Hopefully, Lilly would find a color photo somewhere else.

"You must have loved each other a lot." She gently
touched their faces. They gazed at each other as if no one
else in the world existed. "I want that someday."

Lilly sorted through more papers. The last thing in the
box was an obituary. The date was less than a year before her
parents' marriage.

"Oh." Things fell into place. Her mom and grandma had
been grieving when they had their fight. It probably made
everything worse. She grabbed her phone and texted Abby.

Found Grandpa's obituary. Wish I could have met him.

She didn't expect a response, but she woudn't stop trying.

The cool air finally reached her, sending a chill through
her as it swept over her sweat-soaked clothes. Lilly shivered
and put the newspaper down. She felt hot and cold, sad and
happy, and her stomach growled to top it all off.

"Time for a break." She flipped the air unit off and
grabbed her purse. She'd find somewhere to eat, then get
back to her shopping. Could she stop to visit Flo again?
Would twice in one day be too pathetic?

Lilly had never been on her own. There were always
siblings or friends around. Part of her found the quiet relaxing, but she could only take so much before feeling the
gaping void of the absence of others.

Her phone vibrated in her pocket. Her disappointment it

wasn't Abby faded when she saw her favorite baby sister calling.

"Selena, *mi hermanita favorita*."

"*Chica*, what have you done? Mama wouldn't even say your name when I called at lunch."

Lilly stopped mid-stride. "Really?"

"Papi said you're in Arkansas. Something about a long-lost grandma."

"Not lost, just hidden." Lilly sank back onto the couch. "Aren't you mad?"

Selena sighed on the other end of the line. "I was for a moment, but the truth is I'm too busy to worry about it. We can't change the past anyway."

"But she lied to us."

"I'm sure she had a good reason."

"Like what? She isn't talking to me about it, and from what I've learned here, Grandma Connor tried to apologize many times over the years."

"You know how Mama is."

"Yeah. That's what I'm afraid of."

"Then go home. Talk to her."

"I can't. Not yet. Maybe Abby should be worried I'm too much like her."

Selena laughed. "We all know that isn't the case."

"What's that supposed to mean?"

"You're more even-tempered and forgiving than Mama, that's all."

Lilly sighed. "Humph. Are you getting settled in New York? I could use some happy news."

"It's wonderful! I mean, it's a lot of hard work, but when I have time to explore the city, it's amazing. Will you come out for my first performance?" Selena had recently been hired on at the New York Ballet Company, a huge honor.

"When is it?"

"The season opens in September with Romeo and Juliet."

"I'll be there." Lilly felt a burst of love for her sister. "Selena, I'm so proud of you. And thank you for calling."

"I know, and you're my sister. Of course I called."

"The others haven't."

"Have you called them?"

"No."

"There you are. If you want to talk to them, call. They'll pick up."

Selena was right, but it hurt too much that her mama wouldn't answer her calls. What if her siblings stopped talking to her too?

"I can hear you thinking. Stop. Call them. None of us care you inherited some house in the boonies and we didn't. We care about you."

"Thanks, Selena."

~

*N*ate felt agitated and dissatisfied the rest of the day. He went about his job, putting everything he had into work hoping it would relieve his guilt. He hadn't meant to push Lilly so hard about her choices. Her words had stoked his own guilt, and it had been easier to lash out at her.

Family is valuable. The most important thing in life.

Nate believed that. It was all he'd ever wanted—a family of his own. But he'd run away from everything after his wife died, even his parents. They just couldn't understand how much it hurt to be surrounded by all the memories.

By the end of the day, Nate was a mess. He needed his own brand of therapy, and quick. He didn't need to check on

Gypsy or his horse because the staff at Bear Mountain took great care of them both. However, he found it relaxed him to brush Mrs. Lilly's horse down at night.

The stables were quiet except for the occasional sighs and sniffs from the horses. Nate left the overhead lights off and headed for the one stall that glowed softly in the otherwise inky darkness. Gypsy had GNB, genetic night blindness, and the light helped calm her. He grabbed the brush he kept on a rope outside the door. The old mare nickered, expressing her pleasure at the visit.

"Hey, girl. How about a good brushing?" Nate greeted her and moved into the narrow space. He let the horse nuzzle up to him, wrapped his arms around her head, and stood there with his face pressed against her neck.

The smell of warm horse, hay, wood, and leather combined into a scent that never failed to soothe him. He might not work as a veterinarian anymore or live on his own ranch, but he'd never tire of that smell. Gypsy leaned her head into him a little more, almost like his old retriever did, but the horse's movement almost knocked him off his feet.

"Okay, okay." Nate started with Gypsy's neck. "I met your new owner."

Gypsy groaned, and a shiver moved through her body as she relaxed to enjoy the brushing.

"She's a little spitfire. I think you'll like her." Nate put more pressure into his strokes, knowing Gyp liked that. "Turns out all my belly-aching was a waste of your time. She didn't know about Mrs. Lilly until this week."

Gyp turned her head to nudge at Nate's pockets.

"Before I leave. Anyway, she isn't as bad as I expected."

Nate stopped talking and just worked. The rhythmic motion he'd done thousands of times didn't require thought, and he found his mind stayed firmly on the woman he'd met.

She really was something. That flame in her eyes when she realized he'd tried to do her in with a spicy burger had been glorious to behold. Then there was that moment in Sparky's when he could have sworn she was glad he was beside her.

Until he went and messed it all up. He was a hypocrite. She at least had a valid excuse for not being a part of her grandma's life. What was his? Plain old fear of pain. He left everything and everyone he'd loved behind so he could hide. Why couldn't he keep hiding?

He knew the answer. It had to do with two women named Lilly.

Old Mrs. Lilly had accepted him when he wouldn't allow anyone else to. The new Lilly was so alive. So full of emotions. She'd made him feel something other than pain.

First it was shame for his pig-headed stubbornness, for judging her before meeting her. And then her smile made him feel hope. She'd allowed him to see her vulnerability. It made him want to help her, maybe even be friends.

Then there was that attraction arcing between them.

"Gyp, I've never seen someone so pretty that I 'bout lose my mind every time I'm around her."

The horse made a rumbling sound as if listening and commenting.

Yep, Lilly Ramirez could be dangerous for someone like him. Is that why he kept pushing her buttons and ticking her off?

No, it was because of the pure visceral reaction that pulsed through him every time he looked at her. He'd have to see her again. There was Gypsy. He'd have to tell her about the horse.

"It's going to be torture helping her, Old Girl, but it'll be interesting to see what she thinks of you." Nate worked his way down a long leg.

Lilly had nice legs. Shapely, strong, reminding him of a dancer. Come to think of it, her arms had been toned as well.

"Wonder what she does to keep her figure looking like that? Cause, let me tell you, from the way she lit into that burger, that woman can eat."

Nate swallowed, remembering how that big bite had taken surprised him. No dainty nibbling from Lilly. At Sparky's she seemed to lose her appetite, but he guessed that was his fault too.

She hadn't seemed to notice everyone watching her at Sparky's. Of course, a woman that pretty was probably used to people staring at her.

Meredith had been just as beautiful, but in a different way. She'd been more of the girl-next-door as opposed to Lilly's slightly exotic beauty. Meredith was tall and blonde, Lilly short and dark. Meredith had made him feel comfortable, safe. Lilly had him tied in flaming knots.

"I miss you, Mere."

He let his mind drift to his life as a veterinarian with a competent woman by his side. Meredith might not have had the degree, but she was every bit as good with animals as he'd been. The fact she knew how to act around them made her death even more unbearable.

Nate brushed harder. Meredith never should have been behind the horse in the first place. The hurt turned to anger, burning as it built up in his chest. He threw the brush as hard as he could at the door.

Gyp snorted and danced away from him, bumping into the sidewall of the stall.

"Sorry, girl." Nate grabbed her neck as he fought to calm his voice and the tenseness in his body. "I'm sorry."

Gypsy allowed him to hug her giant head. They stood there a long time until Nate's heart stopped hammering the pain to every part of his body. He had to lock the memories away.

Especially the image of his pregnant wife dying in his arms. Nate knew he'd never survive that kind of torture again. It was why he couldn't let anyone else into his heart.

THURSDAY

*A*fter a full morning of walking through the historic downtown, Lilly wanted to hover in front of the air unit. She stood there with her arms held in the air, soaking in the glorious coolness, when someone knocked on the front door.

"You must be Lilly." Two dark-haired women stood on the porch. "I'm Cheryl Manning, and this is my daughter, Kerri. We knew your grandma from church."

"Oh, please come in." Lilly opened the door and waved them into the sitting room that wasn't full of boxes and papers.

The younger woman, Kerri, pointed to the mess. "I see you've started. Mrs. Lilly kept everything. I interviewed her once for a paper in high school. She made it so easy."

"Really? What did you interview her about?" Lilly sat in the armchair, and the other two took the settee.

"I think it was something about World War II, but it was so long ago I'm not sure." Kerri passed her a plastic container. "I hope you like treats."

Lilly opened the lid and found six yummy-looking truffles in paper cups. The smell of raspberry and mint wafted up. "Who doesn't love chocolate?"

"We're going to be great friends." Kerri laughed, and Lilly couldn't help but join her. "I'm working on opening an experience shop where people make their own truffles. With any luck, we'll be open this fall."

"How exciting. Maybe I'll have to come back when you open."

Cheryl's eyes twinkled. "Who knows, you might change your mind and stay. People tend to do that around here."

"Mom." Kerri rolled her eyes. "Obviously they don't, or we'd be a raging metropolis by now."

Lilly experienced a twinge of longing. Could she stay here? There was a lot of land she could build greenhouses on.

"Eric stayed." Cheryl's smile grew wider, and Kerri blushed.

"Anyway," Kerri rushed on, "we wanted to invite you to church on Sunday. It's where your grandma attended every week. The rest of her friends would love to see you."

"Um, I don't know. I'd feel like I was intruding."

"Nonsense!" Cheryl pulled a slip of paper from her bag. "It's church. Everyone is welcome. Heck, Mrs. Lilly even got Nate Pierce in there once or twice, not that it seemed to do much good. That boy has got a chip on his shoulder."

"Mom, please. We don't know his story." Kerri raised her eyebrows as if trying to drive home some point.

"He seemed okay when I met him." Lilly shrugged.

"I heard he brought you a Diablo burger." Cheryl laughed. "That doesn't sound okay to me."

"He apologized." Lilly felt irritated everyone knew about the burger incident. Sure it was stupid, but he'd been sorry for it. "And I like spicy foods."

"I'm sorry. Kerri tells me all the time I'm a busy-body that needs to know everyone's business. I don't, not really, but that man has been sour ever since he got here, so I can't set him up with anyone." Cheryl laughed and clutched her purse tighter. "He's messing with my matchmaking record."

"Heaven help us." Kerri stood. "Maybe it's good you're not staying long or Mom would try and set you up. My suggestion is run for the hills if she does."

"I don't see you complaining about my insights into the human heart." Cheryl stood too, and they walked toward the door.

"You didn't set me up with Eric," Kerri mumbled. Lilly couldn't tell if she was still blushing or not.

"Not as far as you can tell, but I had my fingers in it, at the very least." Cheryl paused at the door and turned back to Lilly. "Seriously, join us Sunday. We'll save you a seat in our pew."

"Thank you. I'll think about it."

Cheryl patted her arm. "Good. We'll see you around town."

Lilly watched them walk to the car, their chatter drifting back to her.

"Isn't Connor Thomas home? They'd be cute together." Cheryl opened the door.

"Mom, leave it alone, he's dating Regina. Besides, I think they're cousins or something."

"Oh, well, we are in Arkansas…" her words were cut off as she closed the door.

Lilly smiled. They seemed more like friends than mother and daughter. She envied that.

She felt a prickle of curiosity at the possible relative Connor. And why was everyone so concerned with Nate Pierce?

It's none of my business. Get back to the boxes.

44

She decided to eat some chocolate first. Lilly used her phone to snap a picture of them and sent it to Abby. Maybe if she could show her how welcoming the town was, it would help heal the rift between them. Then she could figure out if she had cousins around.

FRIDAY

*N*ate finished loading the mower into the trailer. He didn't get to use the commercial machine often since Eureka Springs was full of trees, rocks, and hills, but he enjoyed it when he could. Mr. Connor watched him as he double checked all the equipment to make sure it was securely tied down for travel.

"Well?" Mr. Connor asked again.

"Why don't you invite her yourself?" Nate used the bottom of his T-shirt to wipe the sweat from his brow. The old man scowled at him. "I mean, she's your grand-niece, sir. She'd probably be thrilled to meet you, so there isn't anything to be nervous about."

"I know, but you've already met her. Belinda said you looked cozy at dinner the other day."

"She did, did she?" Nate removed his ball cap and prayed for the breeze to return. "I've met Lilly twice. I don't know her any better than you do."

"Maybe, but you're closer to her age."

That was true. Mr. Connor wasn't much younger than

46

Mrs. Lilly had been. He was in his seventies, mostly bald, and moved slower than some turtles.

"What's that got to do with you inviting her to Sunday lunch?"

"Nothin', but you're better with people than I am. I don't even talk to my own wife, you know."

Nate shook his head. Everyone in town knew that. They also knew it was because Brandon Connor's wife talked enough for both of them and didn't need him to fill in his scripted part.

"Why don't I go with you, but you do the inviting?" Nate compromised for the sake of his job. He sort of felt bad for the henpecked man, and he needed to tell Lilly about Gypsy.

Mr. Connor rubbed his chin. "I guess that could work. Okay, let's do it now."

"I've got the Mallory job on the other side of town."

"I'll send Joey. He's been asking for extra hours."

"So you're giving him mine?" Nate bristled. Even after two years, he hadn't adjusted to working for someone else.

"No. Bring the equipment, and you can take care of Lilly's fields while we're there. It's about time anyway."

"Okay, but remember, you're doing the inviting." Nate knew it wouldn't work out that way, but he hoped. With another swipe at the sweat dripping from his face, he headed around the truck.

The ride didn't take nearly long enough for him to mentally prepare. Mostly he wondered if he'd find the vulnerable Lilly or the spitfire one. Would she forgive him a second time?

Nate also hoped he didn't react as strongly to her as he had the first two times they'd run into each other. Female entanglements were the last thing he needed. The air shifted inside his truck, and he caught a whiff of that old lady perfume Mrs. Lilly had favored. It sent a shiver down his spine.

"Don't even think about it. Getting caught up in your life is what got me into this mess to begin with. I'm doing what you asked. It's enough."

He swore he heard laughter.

Nate followed his boss out to the house, blasting the air conditioner the whole way. It didn't help, and he continued to sweat like crazy. Darn it all, she was just a woman.

"One I made a fool of myself over." He shook his head thinking about that stupid burger and his accusations at Sparky's.

He needed to start over and put some kind of professional barrier around himself. His job was to help her get through Mrs. Lilly's stuff, introduce her to Gypsy, and help her on her way out of town.

Mr. Connor's car pulled to the left, taking the shade tree as his parking spot. It opened the view to the house where Lilly sat on her knees beside the flower bed. She looked up, using her hand to shade her eyes.

He parked the truck next to her car. By the time he got out, Lilly had moved to the shade of the porch to wait for them. Mr. Connor acted like he'd never spoken to a woman before and practically hid behind his vehicle.

Nate took the lead. "Hi, again."

"Hey, Nate. Who's this?" She waved toward Mr. Connor.

Nate jerked his head toward the porch. "Come on, sir. She might throw something at you, but I promise she doesn't bite."

Mr. Connor's eyes widened like a deer in the headlights. He relaxed when Lilly laughed.

"You deserved it." She waved them forward. "I was about to go in for some lemonade. Want to join me?"

"Sure." Nate ushered his boss forward and spoke low so only he would hear. "Seriously, you've got to do the talking."

"Looks like you're doing fine." Mr. Connor shuffled inside.

Lilly stood by the door. When his eyes adjusted to the darker room, he noticed dirt on her cheek. Her skin glistened from a layer of sweat, and his fingers ached to brush away the hair that had escaped her ponytail to stick to her neck.

Heavens, that neck begged for attention. His gaze drifted down her tank top to the cut off jeans. He admired those perfect legs. When he finally looked her in the eyes, she stared back.

"Done?" she smirked. "Have a seat and I'll bring out the drinks. Maybe then you'll introduce your friend."

Nate could only nod. Seemed he would always look like a jerk in front of her. She left them standing in the hall.

Mr. Connor moved more easily into the next room and sat in the only chair, leaving Nate the smallish couch. He slipped a ten dollar bill out of his wallet and tucked it between the cushions. There, now he'd paid for her lunch.

The sink ran for what seemed like forever. Finally, the fridge opened, closed, and Lilly came back down the hall. She carried three stacked glasses in one hand and a pitcher of lemonade in the other.

She sighed before walking over to the couch. Was she concerned about sitting next to him?

"I didn't think I'd see you again." Her hands and nails had been cleaned, but there was still a smudge on her cheek.

"Why not?" It took more willpower than he thought it should to keep from brushing that little bit of dirt off. "I told you everyone in town would call me if you needed something."

"But I don't need anything." She set the glasses on the table, filled them, and passed them around.

"I might have something that will change your mind." He couldn't help but grin while he struggled to keep his thoughts chaste. It didn't help that she blushed furiously. He plowed on to ease her mind and calm his raging hormones. "I know where you can find some of Mrs. Lilly's relatives."

"Living?"

Nate pointed to Mr. Connor. "This is your grandfather's younger brother."

"Why didn't you start with that?" She set the glass down and hurried over to the silent man. "You're Josiah's brother?"

Mr. Connor stood and held out his hand, but Lilly threw herself into a hug. Nate almost laughed at the man's surprised face.

"Uh, sorry it took so long to visit." Mr. Connor half hugged, half patted Lilly's back. "I don't get out as much as I used to."

"You're here now, that's all that matters. I have so many questions. I want to learn everything about this side of the family." Lilly stepped away, but it didn't look like she was going to sit back down.

Nate stood. "I'll let you two visit while I get to work on the field."

"The field?" Lilly shifted his direction.

Nate swore he could feel her attention like a warm touch. It reminded him of stepping into the glow of a campfire. "Remember, I kept the field under control for Mrs. Lilly. If it gets too tall, you'll have all kinds of critters, and that brings the snakes."

He stepped toward the door.

"Nate, before you go." Mr. Connor tried to give him signals behind Lilly's back.

"Mr. Connor, you do know I was kidding about throwing

things, right?" Nate tried not to laugh. Maybe his boss was shy, but a grown man should be able to ask his family to his house for lunch. "I'll wait while you do it."

Lilly looked back and forth between them, one hand on her hip, a question in her eye. Nate waved at his boss to hurry him along so he could escape to the great outdoors. Even the sun would be better than the heat building under her gaze.

Mr. Connor turned pink. "Well, um. Lilly," he twisted his hands, "my wife and I wanted to invite you to Sunday lunch."

Nate laughed when Lilly danced right there on the spot. Even though the moves were subdued for the space, they made her look even younger, happier.

"I'd love to!"

Nate drifted toward the door.

"Nate," Mr. Connor called to him. "You're invited too. Mrs. Connor has been on me to ask again."

"Thank you, sir. I'll think about it." He nodded his head in their direction and made his getaway to the muggy outside.

*L*illy wondered if Nate would be at church or the Connors' house for lunch. She hadn't seen him since Friday, but he'd never been far from her mind.

She'd found a ten dollar bill in her couch and wondered if he'd left it there. All she could do was laugh and tuck it in her pocket. Mr. Connor had only stayed a short time. He seemed shy and frail, but he had been more than happy to talk about his brother. He'd also mentioned his grandson, Connor, lived in town, and Lilly figured she'd meet him eventually also. When he was ready to leave, she'd walked out to his car with him. That was when she caught a glimpse of Nate on the back of the mower, zipping across the field. In the heat, he'd taken his shirt off and draped it over his head.

"Looks like he forgot his hat again," Mr. Connor commented.

She had a thing for shoulders and abs, and Nate had some of the nicest she'd ever seen. They were well defined, bringing out trails that would be fun to outline with your fingers along his flesh. Lines for tracing from point A to point B to...*Stop it!*

"Uh, I'll see you Sunday. Drive safe." Lilly ran back to the house feeling more hot and bothered than before. Thank goodness Nate hadn't seen her ogling him.

She'd spent the rest of the afternoon going through clothes and knick-knacks, only pausing to look out the window every minute or so.

He caught her staring when he loaded the mower back on his huge red truck, and he waved before driving away. She'd been relieved he hadn't knocked on the door but disappointed too.

Saturday she went for her normal run before the heat got too bad. Lilly didn't run as far as she would at home. The dirt road was mostly flat, but then everything turned to hills. When her legs burned, she headed home and dug back into the boxes.

She was learning a lot about her grandfather, but not much about her grandma yet. There were also things from Abby's childhood. The normal stuff like drawings, handmade cards, school essays. Lilly made piles to donate and piles to ask Abby about. If she ever talked to her again.

Lilly had called and left a message or text every day since she'd arrived. All of her siblings had texted or called, and her papi had talked to her twice, but Abby continued to ignore her. It left her gloomy in spite of her progress at Grandma Lilly's house.

By Sunday morning, Lilly was ready to get out of the house and be around people. She took extra care with her makeup and ran the flat iron through her hair to get rid of the wave from the humidity. Since she hadn't packed a dress of her own, she'd browsed the shops on Spring Street and found a buttery yellow dress with tiny white flowers that hit just above her knees. As she swished the skirt back and forth in front of the mirror, she wondered if Nate would like it.

"Get over it, girl," she chided herself.

Lilly didn't know why she felt so drawn to the man. Well, she did, but usually she moved past the physical attraction quickly and was able to act like an adult. However, she'd barely spent any time with him, and all she could think about was running her hands through his hair and pulling that firm body close.

"Go to church." Lilly pointed at her reflection, then grabbed her purse.

She'd always enjoyed Sunday service. Even though she'd grown up Catholic, she'd attended many denominations with friends over the years. Most places of worship brought her a sense of peace and allowed her to refocus. That's what she needed now.

She drove to the church without any problems. For once the GPS did its job. Parking was another matter. Lilly finally pulled into the post office lot across the street from the two-story brick structure. She wasn't the only one, but it looked like a lot of the congregation walked to church. The building took up one corner of two streets—the one that went past all the shops and another going straight up a hill. It was strange to see a church with no yard or grass.

Kerri stood on the sidewalk a little to the side of the bright red door, a handsome, dark-haired man beside her. He watched Kerri while she scanned the group of people walking up to the entrance. Lilly felt little flutters. Would anyone ever look at her like that? She sighed and put on a smile the same moment Kerri waved to her.

"You came." Kerri met her at the bottom of the steps and gave her a hug. When she pulled back, she introduced the man. "This is Eric."

The man extended his hand. "Nice to meet you."

Up close he was even better looking, and something about him seemed familiar. "Have we met?"

"I don't think so. Ever been to New York City or North Carolina?" he asked.

"My sister lives in New York, but I've only been once." Lilly shrugged.

"Visit any galleries?"

"We didn't have much time for that."

Eric laughed. "Maybe you saw me on a billboard. I used to be big there."

"Really?" Lilly wondered if he regretted leaving New York but didn't want to ask.

"Do you miss it?" Kerri looked up at him, clearly wondering the same thing Lilly was.

Eric kissed the tip of her nose. "You know I don't."

Lilly barely held in her sigh. *So romantic.*

Kerri didn't look convinced. Instead, she reached for Lilly's hand. "Come on. I'll show you where we sit."

They joined Kerri's parents in their pew, smack dab in the middle of the church.

"I'm glad you came." Cheryl gave her a hug and made room for her to squeeze between her and Kerri. Eric sat on the end.

Lilly enjoyed the sermon. The preacher wasn't a yeller, allowing the peace to wash over her. She only got distracted toward the end. Kerri had been rubbing one of her arms when Eric reached over and did it for her.

He massaged it quite thoroughly. Palms, fingers, forearm. He even turned halfway in his seat so he could do a better job of it. Lilly discreetly looked around the room. No one else seemed to notice or care. She figured she shouldn't either, but it seemed awfully intimate an activity for inside a church.

Cheryl leaned over and whispered in her ear. "Kerri has rheumatoid arthritis and that helps with the pain."

"Oh." Lilly blushed with embarrassment. Nothing flirty going on, just a good guy taking care of his girl.

Cheryl simply smiled and reached for the hymnal. After the closing song, Cheryl patted Lilly's arm. "I'm glad you came today, dear. Would you like to come over for lunch?"

"Thank you, but I'm going to the Connors'."

"That's even better! Maybe Nate will be there." Cheryl winked at Lilly, making her drop her purse.

She bent down to grab it and heard Kerri whisper over her head. "Mom, cut it out."

"What?" Cheryl asked, feigning innocence.

Lilly stood and shrugged her shoulders. "Nate was invited but didn't sound like he would come."

She watched a look pass between mother and daughter. It made her more curious about the man her thoughts had been on far too much the last two days. But she wouldn't ask. No matter how much she wanted to.

"I bet he does this time." Cheryl scooted to the end of the pew.

"This time?" Lilly followed.

Before she could answer, Cheryl was distracted by a striking woman in the last pew. Her dark skin contrasted with the white dress, but it was her eyes that kept Lilly's attention. They looked tortured. She almost looked like a ghost hovering in the back as people passed her by without a glance.

Kerri sighed beside her mom. "Excuse me, Lilly."

Kerri pushed her way through the crowd to the woman's side. They stood there talking for a little bit until the crowd broke and they could slip through the front door. Cheryl, her husband, and Eric all exited the building. Feeling forgotten, Lilly walked the aisle alone, wondering what the black woman's story was.

"Hello, you must be Lilly." A group of three older women intercepted her. "We're so glad you're here."

"Thank you."

"We're the Hanes sisters. You know, like the movie?" One of them pointed around their semi-circle, then she sang while waving her hands back and forth. "Sisters, sisters, never were there such devoted sisters."

"Margaret, not in church." Another sister slapped the first woman's arm while rolling her eyes.

"Mary's right. It's embarrassing. Plus, she's too young to remember that movie."

"Age has nothing to do with a classic, Melissa, so hush." Margaret retorted.

Lilly wanted to laugh at these comical women. They wore matching navy blue dress suits with white blouses and bright red hats covered in flowers. Bickering among themselves, she thought they looked like a bunch of puppies fighting over a chew toy.

Margaret shushed her sisters again before turning back to Lilly. "Anyway, we wanted to say welcome and let you know how much we miss your grandma. She made the best coconut cream cake I've ever eaten. If you run across her recipe, would you consider sharing it?"

Mary gasped. "Is that why you were so gung-ho to meet the girl? Shame on you!"

"She might not see it as a family secret. It doesn't hurt to ask." Margaret looked a little ashamed though.

"I'll think about it. I've got to go, but it was nice meeting you ladies." Lilly tried not to smile too big as she waved and rushed to the door. If anyone else stopped her, she might be late for lunch. She glanced back at the three already in another warm if not heated conversation. Maybe she could look the Hanes sisters up to get more information about her grandma.

~

*T*he Connors lived down a narrow and windy road. At least this one was paved. Trees surrounded the place, and a tall clump of bamboo separated it from the house next door. It was an old Victorian painted in shades of yellow and red. It had been well maintained but looked like it was due another coat of fresh paint.

Lilly wasn't sure the color scheme worked, but it looked festive, if nothing else. Several cars and trucks were parked along the road and in the drive, but she didn't see Nate's ridiculously big truck anywhere.

The disappointment surprised her. Well, not really. Mostly she was annoyed she'd been more excited about the prospect of seeing him than meeting more of her family. He was a mystery, and she loved mysteries.

Plus, there was that moment at the diner when he had been her comfort, her grounding stone, so to speak. It had been brief, but for a moment she thought he might understand her. If only he'd stop blaming her for things she had no control over.

She shook her head. "Okay, forget him and go meet the family."

Before she reached the porch, she heard his familiar voice call her name. A strange tremor ran through her, and she turned to him almost against her will. He looked nice. Better than nice. Clean jeans with a pale green button-up shirt. He looked downright sinful. Lilly sucked in a much-needed breath. *What is wrong with me?*

"Glad I caught you before you went in." Nate looked completely unfazed by her. "I wanted to warn you about Mrs. Connor. Her husband is one of the nicest people you'll meet, but his wife." He scratched the back of his neck. "She's more difficult."

"Oh?"

"I just didn't want you to take it personally." He dropped his hand from his neck and stared at their feet a moment.

When he looked up, his gaze took a leisurely trip up her body. Lilly felt the heat of that perusal from the tips of her toes all the way to her lips.

She lost all ability to speak. She stared at him and wished he'd step closer.

He stepped back instead. "I'd better get going."

"Wait." She practically leapt forward to grab his arm. "You drove all the way here, and now you're leaving?"

Nate turned his arm in her hand and moved just enough he could slide his hand into hers.

"I don't do social very well." He spoke softly.

Lilly felt a tremor move through her. Something tangible and fragile hovered between them. She looked for the words to get him to stay so she could figure out what it was.

"Me either, but we're both here. How bad could it be?"

Before he could say anything, an older woman stepped onto the porch, the screen door slamming shut behind her. "Bout time you got here. Stop all that hand-holdin' and git in here so we can eat."

Nate grimaced. "Pretty bad. Guess we're both trapped now."

Lilly didn't know what to think. She looked at the woman with bluish-gray hair piled on top of her head. She wore a loose dress that looked more like a giant shirt than anything else and bright pink glasses.

"Honey, that man ain't spoke ten words to any woman within twenty years of his age for the last two years. Drag him on in here and see if you can hold on to him." She wagged a finger in their direction.

Lilly dropped Nate's hand. "I wasn't, we weren't."

Her gaze darted back to Nate. Why didn't he talk to the

women in town? He gave her a bitter smile and put his hand on her back, gently pushing her forward.

"Might as well get this over with." When they reached the top of the porch, he nodded to the woman. "Afternoon, Mrs. Connor."

"Figures you'd settle on an out-of-towner. What's wrong with our homegrown girls?" She put her hands on her hips.

Lilly froze. Nate removed his hand from her back. She could see how tense his shoulders were, how he already leaned away from the house. He was going to bolt.

"Ladies, thank you for the invitation, but I can't stay. Too much to do." He tipped an imaginary hat in their direction. "See you around."

Lilly actually hurt for him as he stomped across the yard and down the street to his truck. She only wished she knew why.

"That man's more skittish than any critter I've ever seen. Guess you don't have it either." Mrs. Connor shook her head and opened the door.

"Have what?" Lilly tried to tamp down her irritation.

"Whatever it is he wants. Now come on, the food's gittin' cold."

Lilly glanced down the street once more to watch the big red truck disappear around a curve.

MONDAY MORNING

$\mathcal{N}$ate wandered through the aisle of plants feeling lost. Eric Hunt hired Connor Landscaping to work miracles at his house. He'd bought the place in February and started renovations in March. Landscaping was an afterthought, but he wasn't sparing any cost to impress Kerri Manning. From what Nate had seen, that wasn't necessary, but he remembered that feeling of young love. The desire to give someone everything before they even knew they wanted it.

Unfortunately, Mr. Connor's regular landscape designer was out of town on vacation. He thought since Nate had helped with the memorial for Aiden, he could do something like this.

That had been all Brynn and Jaya, though. They had known what they wanted.

He stopped in front of some little blue flowers, rubbing his sweaty hands down his jeans. One plant was pretty much like another, right?

"Seems I can't get away from you."

He spun around to see Lilly standing behind him. She had

haunted every waking moment since he left her at the Connors.

"What are you doing here?" He cringed at the accusation in his voice.

"I needed a break from the sorting. Nurseries are my happy place." Lilly scanned the plants.

Nate had to admit, he'd never seen her this calm. Granted, he hadn't said much yet. And he'd managed to keep his eyes on her face, but just barely. A flicker of a glance was enough to know cut-offs were made for a body like hers. When he spoke next, he made sure his voice sounded more normal. "So, you're just walking around?"

"Is that a problem?" Her eyes twinkled.

"Not at all. It's just not what I'd think of as relaxing." Nate slid his hands into his pockets, anxious not to offend the woman in front of him. "What do you like about it?"

She sighed deeply. "Everything. The colors, smells, even the heat beating down. It just feels good, you know?"

He thought about his love for the stables. "Yeah, I get it."

"So what are you doing?"

"New project. I'm supposed to get plants for a front and backyard, as well as a water feature." Nate tore his attention from Lilly and tried to refocus on the plants. "I'm trying to figure out where to start."

"Do you have a photo of the house? A plan?" Lilly's eyes were bright, the excitement fairly pulsing around her.

"Um, no."

"No wonder you look confused. Want some advice?"

"Sure." Nate couldn't believe she was offering to help him. Not after all the times he'd insulted her since they met.

"Okay. First, we need to go look at the space. I need to see what kind of sunlight it gets as well as a feel for how many plants you need."

"You want me to take you to the client's house?" Nate

rubbed the back of his neck. He probably should have thought of looking at Hunt's yard. Why couldn't Mr. Connor let him stick to mowing?

"Well, yeah. That's the only way to start planning." Lilly put her hands on her hips and squinted up at him. "For a landscaper, you sure are clueless about this stuff."

"I, uh, well, I'm more into mowing, edging. You know, basic stuff."

"I can see that. Come on, then. I'll even let you drive." She winked at him like that was a big deal.

Nate's shoulders relaxed. If she could joke around, he didn't need to worry. She was probably bored at the house all alone.

"You're on. And I've heard how you drive. You couldn't pay me to let you drive." Nate led the way to the parking lot.

"Better watch it or I might rescind my goodwill." She laughed, proving she was still in a playful mood.

"Rescind? Now you're just showing off." Nate smiled.

When they reached the truck, he opened her door. Lilly paused a moment as if she wasn't sure how to climb into the thing. She looked tiny next to it.

He scratched the back of his neck. Suddenly the truck that had already been fitted with a lift kit didn't seem like a good idea. Lilly was so short she needed a ladder just to reach the sidestep up to the truck.

Well, there was an easy fix for that.

"Here you go." He lifted her by the waist and set her inside.

"Whoa, there!" She glared at him, blushing. "What are you doing?"

"I'm sorry." Nate backed away. "I thought you needed help."

"No, but thank you anyway." Lilly shook her head, but her lips softened. The same lips he'd found himself staring at each time they met. "For the record, ask before you pick a girl up."

"For some reason, I can't think straight around you."

"Oh?" Lilly's brow quirked upward.

Nate pushed away from the door, closed it, and took his time walking around the truck. He needed to get it together. And he needed to stop saying stupid things.

I can't think straight? It's like he'd never been to college or run his own successful business. His mind went into drool-mode around her.

Something about her sucked him in every time. Now he had the added problem of knowing how small her waist was and how easy it would be to sweep her off her feet and carry her anywhere he wanted. And his body knew exactly where he wanted to carry her.

He buckled his seatbelt and took a swig of his coke. Then he cranked up the air conditioner, facing the vents at his overheated body.

Lilly didn't seem to notice, but her conversation helped him refocus. "Who's the client? Anyone I might have met?"

"Probably not. It's Eric Hunt, a sculptor from New York."

"Kerri's boyfriend?"

"How?" Nate couldn't believe it. Of course, he shouldn't have doubted that someone like her would get out and make friends quickly. "Do you already know everyone in town?"

She let out a beautiful laugh that was quickly becoming one of his favorite sounds. "No. Kerri and her mom invited me to church, and I met several people there. Eric was one of them."

Nate grunted. Of course she had gone to church her first week in town.

"You know, this isn't the best time of year for planting. It's too hot." She fanned her face.

"I'm just doing what I'm told. I think a lot of his land is

shaded." He glanced at her. She was too hot for little old, geriatric Eureka Springs. Her pale blue T-shirt contrasted with her tanned skin. "It's nice of you to help. I'll have to find some way to repay the favor."

"Hmmm, I bet I can think of something." She smiled at him from across the cab.

His thoughts scattered in at least twenty inappropriate directions. Man, it had been too long. However, she didn't look like the summer fling sort. He'd never been that type either, so he had to get himself under control and fast.

～

It took all Lilly had not to laugh again. Nate Pierce was as easy to read as the billboard for zip-lining they passed. She wasn't usually so bold with her flirting, but watching him struggle to control his attraction was good for her ego.

When Mrs. Connor declared Lilly didn't have what it took, Lilly decided to flirt with Nate until she broke down his walls. After that, well, she'd decide when they got to that point.

"Do you have a timeline for this job?" she asked.

"This week? Mr. Connor isn't big on talk. I'm sure you figured that out at lunch. He just gives general directions and prays we get it done."

"It's a wonder he's still in business." Lilly couldn't imagine being so relaxed with a client's wishes, and she'd only handled flower arrangements.

"Well, as I mentioned, landscaping is generally simple around here. Retaining walls for the hills, plants, or rocks. Most people prefer the natural look because it's easy to take care of."

"So why is Eric going all out?"

"Uh." Nate rubbed the back of his neck in that way she was starting to associate with his being uncomfortable. "His girl, if the rumors are correct."

A little thrill pierced her heart. "That's beautiful. It's why I love flowers so much. They're always associated with love."

"What about funerals?" He scowled.

"Especially then."

Nate pulled into a driveway. The house sat kiddy-corner from the road with plenty of parking. It looked like the hardboard siding had recently been painted. There were also logs on the bottom half of the house, giving it a country cabin look. A separate, modern-looking building sat close by.

"Mr. Hunt redid the second building completely. It houses his studio and showroom." Nate turned off the truck. "Wait here."

"Okay." Lilly watched him walk around the truck to her door. She was surprised when he opened it. "I thought you were going to knock on the door or something."

"I can tell he isn't home. No car." He smiled and waited for her to unbuckle.

Then he took her hand while she slid from the truck. Lilly ended up standing much closer to Nate than was good for her health. He smelled of soap and something she couldn't name, but no cologne. She liked it.

"Thank you." They stood, staring at each other, not moving until Lilly pulled her hands free. "We should get started."

"Yeah. This way. We'll start in the back." Nate led her down a path between the two buildings.

The small backyard ended at the base of a hillside. It was shaded with little pockets of glimmering sunshine falling through the leaves. Creeping ivy had taken over, crawling over the hill and what used to be a pond. Lilly pulled out her phone and took several pictures.

"This has so much potential. Did Eric give you any ideas?" She moved to a different angle and snapped more photos.

"Just that he wants to utilize the pond, add a water feature, and build a firepit or something." Nate's gaze followed her as she moved across the yard.

Lilly put a little extra sway in her hips. The slight motion immediately brought music to mind. Knowing Nate watched made her want to dance for him.

"*No juegues con fuego*," she muttered under her breath, but she could feel the fire building.

"What's that?" Nate followed her to the end of the lawn.

The look in his eyes made Lilly want to fan herself again. She knew she shouldn't, but Nate made playing with fire sound like a good idea. "Nothing."

"You sure?" His brow arched upward, and he gave her a devilish little grin.

"Yep." She swallowed and headed back around the house. So much for bravely flirting. "Let's get photos in front, then we can go back to the nursery."

"You said your sister is a ballerina. Did you ever dance?" He kept pace, not letting her escape.

She could hear a sexy Latin rhythm pulsing through her veins. Heaven above, just his voice made her want to move. "Never ballet."

He grabbed her hand, stopping her retreat. "What kind of dancing were you into?"

A bit of courage returned. Or was it desperate attraction? Whatever it was, Lilly stepped closer, taking both of his hands in hers. She lifted them to chest level, palms next to her palms, and moved even closer before falling into a basic *salsa* step.

"What kind of dancing do I look like I'd enjoy?" She watched his Adam's apple bob as he swallowed.

"You're going to make this hard, aren't you." His hands slid to her hips, stopping their motion, leaving her hands to rest on his chest. "Don't start a *fuego* you aren't willing to put out."

"You know that word?" Lilly liked the way his hands felt on her body. She also liked how strong his muscles felt under her fingers.

"I've been trying to brush up on my high school Spanish."

"Why's that?" She let her fingers trail along his collarbone, over his shoulders, and down his arms. Yes, he was nicely built.

"Let's just say I've been motivated to better myself lately." He leaned closer, never letting his gaze drop from hers.

She recognized the silent question and stretched on her tiptoes to answer.

"Hello? Anyone back here?"

Nate stepped away with a sigh. "Back here, Mr. Hunt."

Eric and Kerri both walked around the corner of the house. Lilly hoped she didn't look as hot as she felt at the moment.

"Please, call me Eric."

"Lilly, I didn't expect to see you. What's going on?" Kerri smiled and looked between Lilly and Nate.

"Uh, we were just..." Lilly searched for an explanation.

"I ran into her at the nursery," Nate interrupted. "She's really into plants and offered to help me with..."

"That's great, but why are you in my backyard?" Eric waved his hands behind Kerri's back, giving the kill sign.

"We were . . . " Nate rubbed the back of his neck again.

"Nate remembered there used to be a pond here." Lilly pointed behind them. "He thought it would inspire us for a project he's working on."

"That old thing?" Kerri laughed. "It used to be amazing years ago. Jen and I would stop here to sell cookies. The woman would always invite us back to see her koi. She even kept a heating unit for the winter. It's not much to look at now."

"You never told me that." Eric wrapped his arms around Kerri from behind. "I keep forgetting you know more about this house than I ever will." He smiled and rested his chin on her shoulder.

Kerri leaned into him. "Hey, you guys want to come in?"

"No thanks, I've got to get back to work." Nate shrugged. "And get Lilly back to her car."

"Yeah, he sort of kidnapped me." Lilly felt the envy rising again. It was clear Eric adored Kerri. Why couldn't she find a guy like that?

"You came willingly because you're bored." Nate's voice jolted her back to reality.

Kerri's brow shot up. "If you're bored, you can help me. I need two more guinea pigs."

"What for?" Lilly tried to focus on the conversation as they strolled to the front yard.

"My new business venture." Kerri outlined a sign in the air with her hands. "Chocolate Dreams."

"Sounds yummy. Need me to taste test something for you?" Lilly asked.

"Sort of. My shop will be more of an experience. That's why I'd need both of you." Kerri winked at Eric before turning a sly smile toward the other two.

"I never said I was bored." Nate shoved his hands in his pockets. "I've got work."

"We can do this when you're not at work. Don't you even want to know what it is, Nate?" Kerri asked.

Nate looked at Eric. "Do I?"

"Trust me, you'll enjoy this." Eric laughed, making Lilly nervous. "It can be...stimulating."

Kerri slapped Eric's arm. "Behave. It's a candy-making

class. I teach you how to make truffles, fudge, cake pops, whatever it is you'd like."

"That doesn't sound so bad." Nate opened the truck door for Lilly.

"It sounds fun. Just let me know when." Lilly didn't move to get in.

"Well, it's sort of a couples thing. You'd have to be available at the same time." Kerri's eyes glittered.

Lilly glanced at Nate. He looked as surprised as she did. Had they seen how close they were standing in the backyard?

"We're not," Lilly started.

Nate added, "We're just friends."

"Uh huh. That's okay." This time Kerri winked at Lilly. "Good chocolate takes patience and care. How about this Friday night? I'll get a few more people to join us."

Lilly only had to think about it for a moment. Helping Kerri sounded like fun, plus she'd always had a weakness for anything chocolate. If it meant more time with Nate, even better. At least they would have Kerri to chaperone. After the almost kiss, Lilly was pretty sure they needed one.

"I'll do it." Lilly peeked up at Nate. *Please say you'll do it.*

His gaze pierced hers, and she wondered if he'd heard her silent plea. "Oh, all right. What time?"

Kerri squealed. "You won't regret it, I promise."

*N*ate worried about the awkward silence all the way back to the supplier. He didn't think Lilly was upset, but she was more subdued than during the trip to Hunt's. If they hadn't been interrupted, he would have kissed her in the backyard.

And then what?

"You're quiet." He kept his gaze on the road, knowing he only had five minutes until they reached the parking lot and her car.

"Sorry, just thinking." She tugged on the seatbelt and shifted in the seat to look at him.

"About?"

"Things. Yards and landscaping." She gave him a coy smile.

"And?"

She laughed, then stopped abruptly. "I'm sorry. It isn't funny, and I should apologize."

"Why?"

Lilly pointed back and forth. "This thing between us. I

don't know what it is, but I shouldn't have teased you. I'll be leaving in a week or two, and it's not fair. To either of us."

Nate felt a twinge of regret, but she was right.

"I know." He pulled into the parking lot, right beside her car. "I've been telling myself the same thing."

They sat in silence, the AC blasting until Nate finally turned the truck off. He hesitated another minute before opening his door. A hand on his arm stopped him from getting out.

"Nate?"

"Yeah?" He didn't turn around.

"Can I still help you with this project?"

He looked over his shoulder to see the question in her eyes. "You really want to?"

"Yeah." She glanced down for a moment, then back up. It made her look pretty in that sweet teasing way she'd just apologized for. "It's what I want to do with my life. At least, I think it is. This would be a good chance to see if I'm any good at it."

Nate relaxed in the seat so his back was no longer facing her. "Sure, but on one condition."

"Yes?"

"You let me help at Mrs. Lilly's."

Her eyes rounded a moment before she glared at him. "Are you trying to get rid of me faster?"

This time Nate laughed. "No, ma'am. I just miss her and don't have anywhere to hang out in the evenings now she's gone."

"Oh. Okay then, but what about," she waved her hands again, "this attraction."

"Honey, we're both adults. We've controlled ourselves so far. We can keep on doing that."

A little crease appeared on her forehead, but she quickly wiped the frown away. Lilly took a deep breath and squared her shoulders. "Agreed. Let's go shopping for some plants."

Nate blinked at the quick change in subject. "You know what we need already?"

"I told you I was thinking about things *and* yards and landscaping." She let his arm go and turned to her door.

"Let me." Nate exited his side and rushed to hers.

"I thought we were going to keep some distance between us?" She gazed at him, and Nate realized this was going to be way harder than he thought.

"I can open a door without touching you." He could, but it might just drive him crazy.

Lilly grinned. She reached up to the hand grip for support, her rear sliding off the seat and her feet hitting the ground. "And I managed to get out of your monster truck without breaking a leg."

Nate knew Mrs. Lilly would be proud of the smile he wore. It had only taken a few interactions with her grand-daughter to make it natural again. "You know, you have a lot of your grandma's humor."

"I do?" Lilly grabbed his arm again.

He was glad she couldn't keep her hands off him. It filled his need to touch her without him breaking his word.

"Yeah. Now, what plants do we need?" He put his hand over hers and led her back into the nursery.

"You trust me?"

"I'm pretty sure you know more about this stuff than I do."

"All right then, let's do this."

Nate let her lead him around for the next hour. He enjoyed the way she touched each plant, almost like she needed to feel if it was the right one. Lilly smelled them all, even the ones without flowers.

"Why do you do that?" he asked.

"You don't want a stinky one, do you?"

"I didn't know plants got stinky."

"They most definitely do. Even some flowers."

She talked about different plants, and he watched her face. Lilly practically glowed in the sunlight. Her eyes danced over each leaf, each bud. When she found something she liked, he'd put it on the pallet. There was no doubt she loved what she was doing.

He shivered.

"What's wrong?" Lilly reached for his arm again but stopped short of touching him. "Am I talking too much?"

"Not at all."

"Then what is it? You looked," she turned away from him, "disgusted."

Nate put two and two together. "Wait a minute. You don't think that had anything to do with you, do you?"

She shrugged and moved to another bush.

"Lilly." This time he allowed himself to take hold of her arm. Once he had both of her shoulders so she faced him, he continued. "What you saw had nothing to do with you. It was about me."

"Okay."

He sighed. "Watching you, it reminded me of something I lost."

"And that hurts?"

"Yeah."

"I'm sorry." She didn't move away, and he could see how her eyes took him in. "What did you lose, Nate?"

Images and memories raced through his mind. Some pleasant, but too many carrying pain. He didn't want to think about it, much less speak it out loud. If he admitted to one thing, it would lead to all of it. "I don't want to talk about it."

"Can I use my one personal question? I told you some-thing no one else knows. I'd like to know this." She didn't demand. Her voice was soft, and something in her tone let him know he could say no if he wanted.

The strange thing was, he wanted to tell her. Needed to tell her. It would be one more layer of protection between them. She was too smart to get involved in someone so damaged.

He picked the least painful and the most relevant thing for the moment. "I used to have a career I loved as much as you love this. I miss that feeling."

Lilly searched the nursery before pulling him across the aisles. She stopped at a bench under an awning. There was a little shade, and the fountains behind the bench added the soothing sound of trickling water.

"Tell me about it. What do you miss the most?" She squeezed his hand, giving him all of her attention.

Heavens, she was about the most perfect woman he'd ever met. A twinge of guilt dragged a ragged breath from his throat. How could he think that after all he'd shared with Meredith? The turmoil churned. Mere had been his perfect woman. She'd known everything, understood him so well, and she'd always stood beside him. She deserved his loyalty.

Nate fisted his hands and stared at nothing.

"Nate?" Lilly whispered. "You don't have to tell me."

He stood. "Look, we'd better finish this up. I have a few more jobs to get to today."

"Okay." Lilly wore a hurt expression, but there was nothing he could do about that.

"Do we have enough plants to get started? I can pay for them, and you can get back to whatever you had planned today." It was getting harder and harder to look at her. She'd been so happy, and once again he'd ruined it with his bad mood. Yet more proof they were better off away from each other. "I'll pick you up tomorrow morning before heading to Eric's."

75

"We've got plenty to start with." She got up from the bench. "I guess I'll go then. Thanks for letting me hang out today."

Nate nodded, turned away from her, and headed back to the pallet of plants they'd left several rows over. He didn't turn around, silently cursing himself for being a jerk but knowing it was the right thing to do.

~

*L*illy watched Nate walk away. Again. She was getting tired of his hot and cold act, but she also ached to follow him. A fire raged between them, but he'd obviously been hurt. She suspected it was more than the loss of his job.

She sighed. One step at a time. If he came around, she would enjoy his friendship. If not, well, she would leave eventually anyway. After one last deep breath of perfumed air, she returned to her car. She didn't feel like going home though.

It was too hot to run, which is what she really needed to do, but a walk up the hill of shops would be good exercise too. As she drove back, she noticed a shop she hadn't seen yet on the edge of town. It appeared to have a little fenced-in garden beside it.

Lilly parked and walked over to lean against the wrought-iron fence. The small yard was mostly a hill, but the flowers ran wild. It was exactly the kind of place she liked. A sign said to visit the springs inside.

"Interesting." She had to take a look. The bells rang as she pushed her way in. There were eclectic and colorful lights, artwork, and knick-knacks everywhere. The shop also smelled of candles or fragrance satchels, but she didn't see a spring.

She moved to the next room and found the display of candles and scented wax melts. A young woman with long, wavy red hair stood behind the counter.

"Excuse me," Lilly said, "the sign said there's a spring somewhere."

The girl smiled and set down the trinkets she'd been sorting. "There is."

She gestured behind her, and Lilly half-turned, looking around handmade glass wind chimes and metal wall hangings. Behind her was a wall of windows and to the side, a doorway into another room.

She gasped. Natural light filtered through the glass; vines and plants brought the craggy rock wall beyond to life.

"It's beautiful," Lilly murmured and stepped into a room with a low rock ceiling arching out from a little cave set against the far wall of the narrow space. The little spring cooled the room and lent the happy sound of trickling water.

No other people were in the shop. Lilly moved close to the rail to let its peace wash over her. How nice of the owners to share this with everyone. She was sure she would have made this her bedroom and kept it only for herself.

Nate's face flashed through her mind, but she quickly banished him. She took a deep breath of the fresh air with a hint of dirt and moss floating on it. Then she pulled out her phone and snapped a picture.

Someone tapped her shoulder, and Lilly jumped. The red-haired sales girl stood there, her hand extended.

"I'm sorry," Lilly stammered, "are pictures not allowed?"

"Sure." The girl pulled her hand back. "They're fine. I just," she rubbed a finger along her nose as if she were searching for glasses to adjust. "I just wondered if you'd like me to take a picture of you with the springs?"

"Oh, thanks." Lilly handed her the phone.

The girl snapped a photo and handed the phone back.

Her gentle smile was almost as soothing as the spring. "There you go."

"Thanks. Could I get your name?"

"It's Sarah." The girl focused on the floor and blushed. "If you need anything else, let me know."

"Thank you, Sarah."

Sarah returned to the desk, and Lilly sent the photo to her family. Most of her siblings replied with some comment before she finished paying for her wax melts and warming pot that looked like a lotus flower.

There was no response from Abby.

TUESDAY

*L*illy hardly slept. Her mind kept jumping from one thought to the other, keeping sleep at bay. She was excited to work on Eric's yard and anxious about her mom. Every time she started to brood over the fact her mother still hadn't talked to her, she refocused on the job. It helped keep her from getting depressed but made for a long night.

She hit snooze several times until five minutes before she expected Nate to arrive. Lilly had just pulled on a pair of lightweight capris to go with her bright red tank top when he knocked. It was seven-thirty on the dot. She swiped her hair up into a pony-tail, bobby pins in her mouth, as she walked down the hall.

"Jus min-nut," she mumbled around the pins and waved him inside.

Nate came in far enough to close the door and waited with his hands in his pockets. He didn't say anything as she moved to the hall mirror and wrapped her hair in a messy bun. She fastened it in place with the pins.

"Okay, ready." Lilly grabbed her keys and pointed outside. "Let's get to work."

Nate stared at her a moment. "I didn't think you'd be ready."

"Figures." She locked up and followed him to his truck, an irrational anger filling her. "You keep trying to fit me in some preconceived stereotype."

"I'm not, I haven't."

Lilly squared off in front of him. "First it was the spoiled absentee granddaughter, and now it's the woman who's always late. You thought I'd be primping and getting dolled up to work in the dirt?"

"Uh, no?"

"Your problem is you think you know me. Truth is, you don't have a clue." She spun and hauled herself up onto the seat, reached out and slammed the door in his face.

Nate walked around the truck slowly. By the time he climbed in, he was scowling.

"What's your problem this morning?" he growled as they rolled down the drive.

"Maybe I'm putting up my own walls. I'm sick of getting sucked into your nice vibes just to be sucker punched a minute later by your grouchiness."

He slammed on the brakes. "You don't have to be here."

"You asked for my help."

"You're the one trying to prove something."

"Arg! Why do you keep coming around?" Lilly unbuckled and practically fell out in her rush to get away. "Forget about the stupid promise you made my grandma. You've done more than enough."

She slammed the door again and stomped toward home. The truck sat still a minute until Nate hit the gas. Tires spun to find purchase in the dirt, raising a curtain of dust between them. Then he was gone.

"*Hombres estupidos!*" Her mind tumbled and swirled all the way home. She'd wanted to work on the yard. Nate didn't know anything about plants, and now he was going to mess it up. "*No vale la pena.*"

She hurried up the porch and yanked at the door. It was locked. Lilly searched her pockets only to realize the keys weren't there.

"Crap." She sat in the rocking chair and took several deep breaths. The only way to fix this was by calming down.

What was her problem? She'd deliberately picked a fight with him for no reason whatsoever.

Several minutes later, she trekked back down the drive. She walked slowly down the middle, scanning the ground for her keys in case she had dropped them. They were probably at the spot she'd left the truck, but she took her time to make sure. She walked well past where they'd stopped before turning around and trying again.

Nothing.

Her keys must have fallen out in the truck itself. "Ug!"

She had two options. Wait for him to find the keys, or call him. Either way, she would have to see Nate at least one more time. Lilly opted to wait. Maybe if she calmed down it wouldn't be so bad when he showed up again. She walked around the house, looking for a way to get inside, but everything was locked up tight.

The anger melted to frustration. If only she'd kept her mouth shut. He hadn't even done anything this morning. Most men thought women were unaware of the time.

Nate had no way of knowing she hated being late. As a child, Abby repeatedly dropped her off late to everything. Everyone would turn to look at the late person. Lilly always felt like they knew she wasn't good enough. That's why she quit dance, soccer, violin, and every other activity as soon as her mom would let her.

"I am good enough." For everyone but Abby.

Lilly sighed. She didn't have her phone, and she couldn't remember if she left it in the house or had it in the truck with her. That's how rattled she'd been when Nate arrived. She couldn't ignore how good he looked.

His hair had called for her fingers to run through it, not yet crushed down by his ball cap or sweat. And when she'd walked past him, she could smell his soap and shampoo. All she could think about was burying her face in his chest and breathing him in. So to protect herself, she'd picked a fight.

She sat in the rocker on the porch again. What was she going to do? She needed to keep busy in order to stop thinking about that good-smelling, good-looking, frustrating man. To top it all off, the temperature kept rising. The humidity already had her sweating and wishing she'd worn cut-offs instead of capris.

Lilly didn't know how much time passed, but she'd practically melded with the chair when Nate's truck flew down the drive. She didn't get up when he stalked toward her.

"Why didn't you call?" he bellowed.

"What?"

"You should have called as soon as you realized you didn't have your keys." He unlocked and threw open her front door.

"I wasn't sure they were in your truck." She couldn't move. Her body was too tired. "And I didn't have my phone."

"It's almost a hundred degrees." He took her by the elbow and helped her stand.

"Whoa." Lilly latched onto him.

"Are you dizzy?"

"A little."

"You're dehydrated." He scooped her up into his arms.

"Nate, put me down. I'm fine." Even she didn't believe her words. Her head found the perfect resting place on his shoulder. The soap smell wasn't as strong, and now he smelled more like the dirt and sweat she was liking more and more. *So weird.*

He set her on the couch. "Don't move."

"I can't be dehydrated," Lilly fussed, but laying on the couch felt good. The air was warm but better than outside. She glanced at the wall, surprised to see it was almost eleven. Where had the time gone?

Nate returned with one glass of water and one of lemonade. "Drink these."

She struggled to sit up. "Can you turn the air on?"

He did as she asked, and she started on the lemonade. It was cool and tart, just the way it should be. She giggled. Of course, it was. She'd made it after all.

"You're not going to faint, are you?" Nate sat beside her and reached for her hand. He placed his fingers on her wrist.

"What are you doing?"

"Shh." He sat still, then nodded his head. "Good."

"So I'll live?" She bit back the laugh that wanted to bubble up again. "Did you used to be a doctor?"

"Sort of," he mumbled and pointed to the glass. "Keep drinking."

"How can you sort of be a doctor? Were you a nurse?"

"I was a veterinarian."

"That fits you." Lilly finished the lemonade and slouched down in her corner of the couch.

"You need to drink the water too." Nate helped her sit. "Did you drink anything this morning? What about breakfast?"

"I didn't have time."

He grumbled something unintelligible, then asked another question. "What about last night?"

"I don't know. I've been busy."

Nate shook his head. "Drink more water. This house is

old, and it gets hot. Add the humidity, and you need at least eighty ounces of water a day."

Lilly laughed. "Yes, I can see you now. Hello, Mrs. Cow. It's a fine day, but you're not drinking enough water. Get down to the watering hole right now." She jabbed him in the chest.

"That's not funny." But his lips twitched with a hint of a smile, egging her on.

"You goats are too stubborn for your own good. Get in the barn and take a nap before you pass out from over-exertion." She pointed at him, trying to think of something even sillier to bring out a full smile from him. "You lilly-livered chickens better..." Her hand rested against his broad chest, and her mind went blank. *Oh my...*

"Better what?" he asked with a smirk.

Lilly scooted away and sighed. "I have no idea. Stop laying eggs until the heat wave passes?"

Nate chuckled. "You're really on one today."

"I didn't get much sleep." She shrugged and sipped more water. The pounding in her head eased.

"Why not?"

"Couldn't turn my brain off." She set the glass down and rested her head against the back of the couch.

"Lilly, I'm sorry."

She closed her eyes and waved at him dismissively. "It's my fault. I was cranky and looking for a fight."

"But I was more than happy to oblige." He moved beside her. After a minute of quiet, he spoke again. "I don't mean to make you angry every time I see you."

"I'm sure you don't. Maybe I just bring the worst out of you, like I do with Abby."

～

*H*er words hit him in the gut like falling out of a tree. They stole his breath, filling him with regret. Sure, she pushed his buttons, but he knew none of their arguments had been her fault. Not even the last one.

"You don't bring out the worst in me." He twisted around so he could face her on the couch. She sat with her eyes closed, but she already looked better than she had when he arrived. Seeing her slouched on the porch, pasty-skinned and dull-eyed, had scared him. "Truth is, for the last two years I've barely talked with anyone. My social skills are rusty."

She cracked her eyes open to look up at him. "Rusty, huh?"

"What can I say. Mrs. Lilly was the only person I ever talked to, and she did the talking."

"What did you guys chat about?" Lilly turned on her side, her feet tucked under her legs. She still rested her head as if it were too heavy to lift.

"Here, drink more water." He held the glass out again.

"Fine, but tell me while I do." She took it.

"We talked about your family, mostly. She was always doing internet searches on your names, looking for news articles that might tell her something about your lives. Whenever she found one, she'd read it to me and then talk about it for hours."

"Really? What did she know?"

Lilly's soft smile stirred something in Nate. It had since day one. Why did he keep trying to push away someone so kind? She'd proven time and again how much she loved the people in her life, how much she wished she had met Mrs. Lilly.

"She told me about Joe Jr. getting the ER residency in New York and about Gael joining the Air Force. Last year she was thrilled with the praise Selena got with the San

Francisco Ballet. She was waiting to hear if she was chosen as principal."

"That happened in December, but she turned it down to be a first soloist with the New York Ballet. She moved there last month."

"Mrs. Lilly would have been proud."

"What about Maria?"

"Ah, Maria likes to keep her life private. She was harder for Mrs. Lilly to pin down, but she learned enough to make a donation to her organization."

"Wow." The little crease reappeared on Lilly's forehead. Her lips tilted down, and she put the glass back on the table. "There wasn't much to read about me either. I've never been in the papers."

"I swear that woman learned stuff that should have been impossible."

"What do you mean?"

"She knew every time you changed jobs. You have no idea how thrilled she was you liked to work with flowers. She knew where you lived and where you worked."

That got her attention. She sat up straight. "Wait, she knew that and never wrote or called me?"

Nate squirmed. "She promised your mom she wouldn't contact you."

"That's just stupid. If she'd called or something, I could have met her, maybe helped bridge the gap between her and Abby."

"Maybe." Nate rubbed his thumb over her hand, trying to calm her down. "Maybe she thought the only way to heal the rift was to show Abby she respected her wishes."

Lilly's eyes glimmered, but she didn't cry. "How can a relationship get so twisted? It doesn't make sense."

"I don't know." But he kind of did. He hadn't spoken to his parents since he left home. Pride, shame, fear, all things that kept him from reaching out. He was a coward. "We barely know each other and our relationship is full of knots."

"That's because..." She shut her mouth with a snap and looked away.

"Because?"

"Never mind. All this liquid is getting to me. Excuse me." She got up and fled to the bathroom.

Nate sighed and gathered the cups to take back to the kitchen. He knew what she hadn't said. They were so busy fighting the physical attraction between them, they kept messing up everything else. He put the glasses in the sink and looked for food. Lilly needed to eat something. All he found were frozen meals.

"What are you doing?" Lilly asked from behind.

"I was going to get you some lunch, but this isn't food." He closed the fridge. "Looks like I'm taking you into town."

"You don't have to do that."

"I do. It's my fault you almost passed out on your own porch."

"I think food is your go-to apology. The question is, will I get to eat it?" Her brow rose, and she cocked a hip to one side in what could only be labeled as sass.

"Ouch." Nate took her by the shoulders and turned her toward the door. "I promise to be on my best behavior. If it helps, I'll keep my mouth shut the whole time."

"I'd like to see you eat without opening your mouth." Lilly laughed. "Let me find my phone."

Nate waited while she searched both front rooms before disappearing into the bedroom. When she came back out, she'd changed her pants to shorts. He preferred more clothes so he could think clearer. He'd always been a leg guy, and she had it going on in that department.

"Nate?" she teased. "Really?"

"Sorry, but I think you do it on purpose. Just to torture me."

"Come on." She pulled him toward the door. "That's like saying you mess your hair up like you just crawled out of bed to torture me."

"You think about me in bed?" It was his turn to tease, and he liked the direction of her thoughts. Far too much.

"I shouldn't have said that." She closed the door, locked it, and put the keys in her purse. "Shouldn't lose them this time."

Nate chuckled, glad they were back to an easy-going flirty vibe. He opened her door and lifted her into the truck. She rolled her eyes at him but didn't complain.

"So, how did it go at Eric's this morning?" Lilly asked after he'd reversed out of her drive.

"I dropped everything off in the backyard but didn't get much else done. I left some guys clearing out the old stuff."

"If you want, I could still…" She stopped and looked out the window.

Nate could see her chewing on her bottom lip. "Yeah, I do."

Her head whipped around, and the joy in her eyes lit up his insides.

"Thanks." She beamed at him.

Yeah, he didn't know how much longer he could fight the attraction. Not when she was worming her way into his life with that smile.

"But, we're grabbing lots of water bottles, and you have to keep drinking. At least it'll be mostly in the shade." Nate pulled into Subway. "Hope this is okay, my lunch break is pretty much over."

"This will be fine." Lilly allowed him to help her out of the truck.

Once they had their sandwiches in hand and a couple

water bottles each, Nate drove them to Eric's house. He had to lift her onto the tailgate so they could eat.

"Why in the world do you have such a monster truck?" Lilly asked. "It doesn't seem like your style."

"What do you mean?" Nate had eaten his sandwich in record time and watched her nibble at hers.

"From what I've seen, you don't want people to notice you. This truck screams, 'look at me.'"

"Keep eating." He worried that her appetite hadn't returned yet. Maybe letting her work so soon after sitting in the heat wasn't a good idea.

"I will, but answer my question." She took a large bite as if to satisfy him, raising her eyebrows his direction.

"Good girl."

Lilly rolled her eyes at him.

Nate chuckled. "I don't know. I needed a truck, and this one was for sale. It might not have been my style, but it's grown on me."

"Huh. Guess that's all that matters, then." She took another bite.

"Plus, it's turning out to be a bonus now that I'm talking to girls and giving them rides around town." He bumped his shoulder into hers.

"Nate Pierce, you are something else."

He just grinned, feeling a strange warmth in his chest. It had been a long time since he'd felt this comfortable around a woman.

"Drink that whole thing before we start." Nate nudged a water bottle in Lilly's direction.

"You're sounding like a broken record. Drink, hydrate, I get it."

He knew from her grin she wasn't upset. "We'll work in the back today, then the front tomorrow morning."

"Sounds like a plan." She took a swig of water, wadded up her wrapper, and scooted to the edge of the tailgate.

Nate jumped down first and moved in front of her. He gripped her waist and lifted her down. "How do you do anything being so short?"

"I've managed just fine." She held on to his arms and looked up at him. "Do you bump your head a lot?"

Nate laughed and let go reluctantly. "Come on, let's see if the back is ready for planting."

Sure enough, the guys had cleared everything he'd asked them to. The pond had been emptied and cleaned, the parts for the water feature placed beside it, and all the flower beds had been dug up and fertilized. Unfortunately, that meant he was once again alone with Lilly. Memories of their almost-kiss haunted this place. When Lilly glanced at him, he wondered if she was remembering too.

"Where do we start?" he asked.

WEDNESDAY

*T*he next morning dawned much better. Nate knocked on her door earlier, but he arrived bearing gifts of pastries and orange juice.

"No rush." He shrugged and handed over the goodies. "You can eat them here or in the truck, doesn't matter to me."

Lilly smiled at how accommodating and non-confrontational he tried to be. She also admired his thick, non-hat hair again. Part of her wished he wouldn't cover it up with that ball cap of his. It just begged to be messed up by her fingers. She shook the thought off and set the box on the side table.

"I'll get my phone and my keys and eat in the truck. No use wasting the cooler morning unless necessary. It's supposed to be just as bad as yesterday."

"Good call." He shoved his hands in his pockets.

Lilly grabbed a small handbag big enough for those two items and a small wallet. Then she grabbed the box of what looked to be a mix of doughnuts, puff pastries, croissants, and danishes.

"Are you feeding everyone today?"

"Nah, just didn't know what you'd like, so I covered all the bases." He opened her door and set her on the seat.

Lilly was getting used to him lifting her in and out of his truck. It should bother her. She wasn't a child or a doll, but she loved having his hands around her waist. She'd enjoy what she could get.

Nate walked around the front of the truck, a sure indication he was in a good mood. Lilly had noticed he walked around the back when he was agitated. Probably hoping for an extra second or two to cool off. She tried not to grin at the thought.

The drive to Eric's was quiet because she spent the whole distance stuffing her face.

"Seriously, you've got to stop feeding me. I've gained two pounds this week."

"Why do women worry so much about their weight? You look perfect to me." Nate gripped the steering wheel tighter.

Lilly blushed, but her heart also warmed. "We should finish the back pretty early. Will we start on the front today?"

"Yeah, Eric wants it done as quickly as possible because he doesn't know how long he can keep Kerri from driving by."

"That's why we started in the back?"

"Exactly. And it needed more work."

Lilly took another bite out of a strawberry cream cheese danish. "What's their story?"

Nate shrugged. "I only know what Mrs. Lilly told me."

"I bet she knew quite a bit. She seems like she was a regular detective, from what you've mentioned about my family."

"You're right. Didn't think about that." They pulled into the drive. Nate shot her a quick look, the one that meant "stay in that seat until I get to your door."

Lilly giggled like an idiot but stayed put. Then she let him wrap those big warm hands around her and pull her off the seat and to the ground.

All other thoughts disappeared as she stood in the delicious circle of his arms as long as she dared before stepping away. "Come on, then."

It only took a couple of hours to finish the back, since other guys from Connor Landscaping showed up to help. Lilly watched how Nate interacted with them. He was nice when he gave orders and talked when spoken to, but he didn't joke with them or chit-chat. He was much more open with her than any of them. The realization brought a strange sensation to her chest.

Nate deferred a lot of the managing to her. The men took it all in stride, and she wondered what Nate had said to them. It didn't matter to her, as long as the work moved smoothly. Which it did.

A little after lunch, she gazed over the backyard. It had been transformed, even better than she had envisioned.

"The only thing left is to get the fountain on and fill the pond. We can start on the front while the guys do that." Nate stepped in front of her.

He'd made this possible. Given her the chance to do something she'd always wanted. Emotions deeper than just attraction filled her heart. Why couldn't she feel this way about any of the men she'd dated back home? There had been plenty she liked, but none stirred her the way Nate did. And none had understood this side of her.

"What are you thinking?" Nate asked.

"Nothing." Lilly's face heated. "Okay, what's next?"

His smile told her he knew she'd not been paying attention. "The front yard."

"Right."

They fell into an easy rhythm of work and talk. She finally convinced him to talk about his days as a veterinarian.

He stuck in funny stories about his school years, avoiding the time after that, but his antics were so hilarious, she didn't dwell on that fact. She was laughing at one of the stories when he abruptly stood up.

Lilly turned to see a woman stomping her way across the lawn with an angry twist to her mouth. She was tall and slender with strawberry blond hair, leaning more toward the strawberry, and wide blue eyes. The woman tossed a quick glance behind before reaching them. She was beautiful in that girl-next-door kind of way. Lilly couldn't help but wonder what Nate thought. He hadn't taken his eyes off her since standing.

"Can I help you?" he asked.

"I'm looking for Kerri or Eric. Mostly Kerri." The woman shot a flirty smile in his direction, but it faded quickly. "Are they around?"

"No. Eric will be back this afternoon, but my guess is Kerri won't be around until her surprise is finished." The tension left his shoulders as he indicated the yard and extended his hand. "I'm Nate Pierce."

Lilly tried to swallow the flair of jealousy. *He's not mine.*

"Jennifer Carlson. Kerri's been my best friend since grade school. I just moved back this week."

"Nice to meet you." Nate pulled back and placed his hand on Lilly's back. "This is Lilly Ramirez."

Lilly thrilled at that small gesture. She reached out and shook Jennifer's hand, determined not to give in to the jealousy. "Do you think Kerri will like the landscaping?"

The woman took a long look around. There wasn't much for her to notice yet, just the cleared beds and the new stone border outlining them. "Anything will be an improvement. Kerri loves color, and I'd guess a messy approach."

"I thought so! Something about her made me think she'd like a more natural garden as opposed to everything in regimented lines." Lilly bounced in place, glad she'd picked up on that from her few interactions with Kerri.

"Definitely." Jennifer glanced over her shoulder toward the road again. "Well, I'll leave you guys to it and head on down the street. Maybe I'll catch Kerri at her mom's shop."

"Have a good day." Lilly was eager to put plants in the ground.

Nate nodded, and the woman jogged back to the sidewalk. She didn't seem as agitated as when she'd stormed up to them. Maybe she'd just been concerned strangers were in her friend's yard? Lilly shook her head. There were three Connor Landscaping trucks in the drive.

Whatever. Lilly turned around and stumbled into Nate. "Oh, sorry."

He wrapped his arms around her to keep her from bouncing off. "My fault. I should have known you were too distracted to notice me here."

"Uh, that's not likely." Lilly melted into him, and it wasn't the humidity. "How do you know I didn't do this on purpose?"

His arms tightened, drawing her closer. "Is that right?"

"Hey, Nate." One of his co-workers came around the house. "Oh, uh."

Nate jumped away from her. "Yeah?"

"We needed you to check off the fountain." He didn't say anything about how close they'd been standing, but he gave Nate a thumbs up.

Nate took his ball cap off and scratched the back of his neck before replacing it. He glanced at Lilly. "Want to come and see?"

Lilly grabbed one of the water bottles from the back of the truck. It would take a lot more than a drink to cool off. She picked up a second one and carried them to the back. The shade only dropped the temperature a degree or two.

The sound of water trickling over rocks lent a peaceful sound to the riot of plants, giving the backyard a secret hide-away vibe. She took her time walking to Nate's side.

"Drink?" She held out the water.

His fingers caressed the back of her hand before taking the bottle. "Thanks."

Lilly's body warmed a couple more degrees from that slight touch. They would need to revisit this just friends thing or avoid Eric Hunt's yard.

At least they'd lasted an entire day without arguing about stupid stuff.

~

*N*ate dropped Lilly off at her place around five in the afternoon. He'd gone home to shower and change before joining her at Mrs. Lilly's to go through some boxes.

The rational part of him knew it was a bad idea. Every time he was near her, all he could think about was pulling her close and kissing her senseless. The fact that forty minutes away from her felt like an eternity confirmed that. But he was determined to act like an adult. Keep it under control.

They'd been sorting through stuff for an hour. Other than a box full of vintage dresses, there hadn't been much for Lilly to get excited about.

"You find anything interesting?" Lilly asked.

He held up a paper for her to see. "Not really. I don't suppose you need all these boxes of union papers, do you?"

"What are they, exactly?" Lilly put down the clothes she held and made her way to his side.

Nate could smell the shampoo from her still damp hair. She'd put it up in that bun again. He concentrated on her question to keep from reaching out and setting her hair free. "Statements showing that Josiah paid his dues. They go back to the 1940s."

"Interesting, but I think we can trash them." Lilly leaned over his shoulder. "I didn't realize one person could hold onto so much useless stuff."

"Mrs. Lilly didn't want to need something and find out she'd thrown it away." Nate chuckled nervously. He could feel the heat from her body. His senses were on overload. "She used to fold up the take-out bags to reuse."

"Really? What could she possibly want them for?"

"I don't know. I never saw her pull them out. You'll probably find them when you go through the kitchen." His gaze darted around the room, finally falling on her again. What if she didn't leave Eureka Springs? "What are you going to do with this place?"

Lilly sighed and backed away a step. "I don't know. The smart thing would be to sell it, but this place feels like home."

"You've only been here a week." Nate couldn't decide if he wanted her to stay longer or leave sooner.

Mrs. Lilly? What's best for her? He asked silently, realizing he wanted Lilly to be happy, and her grandma might be the only one able to help.

Lilly scooted to the wall and sat down, making it easier for him to think.

There was no reply from Mrs. Lilly's ghost, not even a hint of her perfume. She'd been quiet lately. Maybe she'd finally moved on.

Nate watched Lilly closely, hoping to untangle his own feelings.

"There's something about this house, this town. The only thing missing is my family." Lilly pulled her phone out and glanced at the screen. Her shoulders slumped, and he guessed she hadn't seen what she wanted. "I wish Abby would come.

If only she could see what her mom kept. She's got all of Abby's school papers and loads of photos."

"You can take them home to her." *Please don't go*. His head and his heart wanted different things.

"I know, but will that be enough?" Her sad expression caused a physical pain inside him.

Nate shrugged, but decided he should say what he'd been thinking ever since he'd met her grandmother. If Lilly got upset, it might be the answer he needed. "It doesn't sound like your mom wants to forgive Mrs. Lilly. If she did, she would have done it a long time ago."

"What does that mean for me?" She held up the phone again. "Complete silence since I left."

Nate's need to touch and comfort her finally won out. He crawled over to where she sat, wrapping her in an embrace. "She'll come around."

She was warm in his arms, and he couldn't help but register how well she fit there. Lilly turned into his embrace, her curves molded to him, making him feel like he could and should protect her from everything that wanted to tear her down. Even her mom.

She rested her head on his chest. "How can you be sure?"

"She's the mother this time. I don't think she'll be able to let you go." *I've only spent a week with you, and I don't know how I'm going to.*

"*Dios, espero que no*," she whispered.

"*Espero*, is that hope?"

"Yeah."

"There's no need to hope." Nate rubbed her back. "She just needs time."

"Am I wrong to stay here? Should I go home and try to fix this?"

Nate barely contained his plea for her to stay. She deserved more than he could give her, and he wouldn't

98

burden her with how much he needed her in his life. "No one can decide that but you."

Lilly pushed off his chest so she could look into his face. "I don't want to leave yet."

Relief flooded his system. He nodded and moved a stray hair off her face. Heavens, he wanted to pull that bun loose, but he kept his hands away from it. "Then stay as long as you need to."

"Thanks, Nate."

"Now, get back to work." He gently pushed her away before he did something stupid. Like kiss her.

She drifted to another box, and he retreated to the other side of the room. After a few minutes, he remembered he still hadn't told her about Gypsy.

"By the way, you have a horse."

"A horse?" Lilly looked up from the box.

"Yeah, she was Mrs. Lilly's. Now she's yours."

"What's her name?" The excitement in her voice bounced around the room. She stared at him, her hands clasped in front of her like a little girl. "I always wanted a horse, but Abby wouldn't let us have one."

"Well, now you do. Her name is Gypsy, and I can take you out to meet her on Saturday if you want."

"Gypsy is a great name. Can we go tomorrow after we finish at Eric's?" She actually batted her eyes at him.

Nate chuckled. "How old are you?"

"Twenty-eight last month, but that doesn't matter when it comes to little girls and their horses." Her smile made up for the unbearable heat of the upstairs room.

Even with the sun setting and the windows open, the house was sweltering. Nate glanced at his watch and wiped his sweaty hands on his pant legs. It was only nine-thirty. "We could go meet her now. Then you could go for your first ride tomorrow."

"Yes!" Lilly scrambled over the boxes in front of her instead of going around. Her mood had completely flipped from earlier. She grabbed his hand and tugged him toward the hall and stairs. "Come on."

He laughed as she dragged him down the steps. She didn't pause at the bottom.

"Gyp is going to like you." Nate allowed her to pull him toward the front door. "Do you have keys?"

"Right." She dropped his hand and hurried to her room. When she came back, she had her tiny purse and had changed into tennis shoes. "Now I'm ready."

Nate helped her into his truck, trying hard to wipe the grin off his face. Her enthusiasm was contagious. It was only a five-minute ride to the stables. Lilly asked questions and fairly bounced in her seat the whole way.

"What kind of horse is she?"

"An appaloosa."

"Those are the ones with spots all over them, right?"

"Yep."

"What color is she?" Lilly turned in her seat so she could face him.

Nate loved how she did that. Like she had to see him in order to talk. "She's a dark brown, almost black, with a white rump. Although she's got quite a bit of gray mixed in now."

"I bet she's beautiful. And I can ride her even though she's older?"

"If I can ride her, you'll be fine." Nate pulled up to a large red barn. "Here we are."

"Nate." Lilly grabbed his arm before he could get out.

He turned to see her gazing at him with a rapt look on her face. If he didn't know better, he would call it adoration. "Yeah?"

"Thanks for this. For everything."

Nate shrugged and left the truck, determined not to dwell

on how much he liked it when she looked at him like that. He couldn't get used to it. Lilly waited for him to open the door, but as soon as he did, she practically fell into his arms.

Lilly didn't take her eyes off of him. "I mean it, Nate. Thanks for being with my grandma, for taking care of her and her horse. You didn't have to do that, and I want you to know I'm grateful."

Friendly, keep it friendly.

But he wanted to kiss her so bad. Instead, he nodded his head and retreated. "Let's introduce you, then."

The barn was just as empty as when he'd last visited. Nate was glad the owners were comfortable with him coming and going as he pleased. This time he flipped on the lights. Several horses poked their heads over the stall door.

"There are so many." Lilly spoke softly.

"You won't spook them. Gypsy is around the corner to the left." He led her to Gyp's stall, opened it up, and stepped in to greet the horse. "Hey, girl, how's your day been?" Gypsy nickered and shuffled closer. Nate slipped a rope around her neck and led her out where there was more room. "Come and meet the new Lilly."

Lilly watched, her eyes round, but she held her body stiller than he'd ever seen.

"You okay?" he asked.

"Can I touch her?"

"Of course. Stay in front where she can see you." Nate held Gypsy with one hand and reached for Lilly with the other. "Give me your hand."

She did as she was told, and he tugged her near enough to run her fingers down Gyp's muzzle.

"She's soft." Lilly inched closer, and Gypsy pressed her head into Lilly's chest. Nate moved behind Lilly and wrapped his arms around her waist to keep her from falling under the onslaught. She laughed. "What does that mean?"

"It means she likes you and is hoping you have treats." Nate liked how Lilly leaned into him and the way her arms gripped his. He paused only a moment before setting her on her feet and stepping away.

His gaze drifted to her lips. There was an awkward pause, and Nate wondered if her thoughts drifted the same direction as his. "Um, want to give her an apple?"

Lilly glanced at him through her lashes. "Yes, please."

"Wait here." He returned to the front, where he knew the owner kept a stash of treats. There weren't any apples, but he found a carrot before heading back.

That was when it hit him that he'd left a horse loose in the barn with a woman who had never been around them before. "Aw, hell."

He jogged around the corner to find Lilly and Gypsy exactly where he'd left them. The woman had draped her arms around the horse's head and stood whispering in her ear. She glanced up before he could get close enough to hear what she said.

"What?" she asked.

"Nothing." He didn't want to admit to the fear that had him charging back to her.

What if Gyp had knocked her down, stepped on her? Meredith had grown up around horses, but that hadn't mattered in the end.

Meredith. He hadn't thought about her in days. Guilt rose like bile in his throat. He swallowed it down and refocused on the moment. He couldn't afford to get reckless with Lilly, and there would be plenty of time to wonder at the change in this thought pattern.

Nate calmed down enough to allow Lilly to feed Gyp the carrot before easing the horse back into the stall. "It's late. We'd better get you home. Early morning and all."

"Okay." She frowned for a moment but quickly changed her expression back to her normal happy one.

He knew she was disappointed at the short visit. They were quiet all the way back to Mrs. Lilly's. It gave him plenty of time to think. His thoughts circled around Lilly, her problem with her mom, and why he hadn't thought about Mere as much lately.

Nate helped Lilly out of the truck and walked her to the door. "I'll see you in the morning. We'll finish up at Eric's, then I'll give you your first riding lesson."

"I look forward to it." Lilly hovered in the door as if she didn't want to go in.

"Lilly?" Nate rubbed the back of his neck, hoping he wasn't about to make her mad again.

"Yeah?"

"What if you stopped calling your mom Abby? She might like to hear you call her mom."

Lilly's face scrunched in thought, and she tilted her head to the side. "You might be right. I'll try it and see what happens. Thanks, Nate."

They stared at each other a minute more until Nate forced himself to back away. He'd made it an entire day without upsetting her. Hurray for him.

~

It was after ten, but Lilly knew it would be a while before she could sleep. She was too happy. Thanks to Nate, she'd been able to spend two days watching one of her designs come to life. It was better than she'd ever imagined. Sure, the work was hard. Her knees hurt from kneeling on the ground, it was miserably hot, and her nails had all broken, but she was doing it.

And she had a horse!

Lilly pulled up her favorite playlist and danced in the front room as she sang along. When she went out with her friends she preferred Latin dancing, but her secret love was country music. Her heart connected with the stories they told.

After two songs she couldn't deny that much of her joy was tied up in Nate. He continued to grow on her. She stopped dancing and grabbed her phone.

"You may be onto something, Nate Pierce." She pulled up her mama's contact and started a text.

Mama, I have a horse! Nate will teach me 2 ride 2mrow. Did U have horses growing up?

She hit send and waited about five minutes. When she didn't get a response, she sent another one.

Sorry. Ur prbly sleeping. Love U.

There. It wasn't much, but it felt good. No more Abby. Just Mama.

"*I*t looks great." Eric stood in his backyard. "Kerri will love this."

"It was all Lilly." Nate smiled down at her, and Lilly thought she would burn up.

Somehow she'd survived four days in a row without kissing him, but she knew it wasn't for lack of desire. The last two days had been perfect. No fighting. Just good conversation, laughing, and flirting that had her tossing and turning at night. The fact he was giving her all the credit for the job in front of Eric was the icing on the cake.

"Look," Eric went on, "I know you're supposed to help Kerri with her chocolate class tomorrow, but I want to bring her here for a reveal party instead. Will you guys come to that?"

"We'd love to!" Lilly grabbed Nate's arm. She glanced up to see his brow arch up. "Oh, sorry. I mean, I'd love to come."

Nate put his hand over hers before she could pull away. "What can we bring?"

Lilly thrilled at his "we."

"Potluck sides, desserts, drinks, whatever you want. I'll

provide steaks and burgers for the grill." Eric pointed to one side of the yard. "I've got someone bringing in some tables and chairs."

"This is going to be so much fun." Lilly couldn't wait to meet more people from town. She'd spent most of her time with Mrs. Lilly's storage room and Nate. Not that she was complaining. "What time?"

"Eight-thirty. Hopefully, it'll start cooling off a little by then."

"That's great. Maybe we can go riding before?" Lilly turned to Nate. Ever since learning she had a horse, all she wanted to do was get out and ride it.

"There should be plenty of time. Especially if your lesson goes well today." His phone rang. "Be back in a minute."

"You did a great job with the yard," Eric said again. "I want this to be somewhere Kerri can spend hours relaxing, and I think she's going to love this."

"I enjoyed doing it." Lilly watched Nate, only giving Eric half of her attention.

"So, uh, you and Nate?" Eric nodded across the yard.

Lilly blushed. "No, why?"

"Kerri keeps asking." He shrugged. "Why not?"

Lilly mimicked his shrug. "I'll be leaving."

Eric nodded. "Is that what you want? When it came down to it, staying made me happier than leaving."

Before she could answer, Nate jogged back to them. "Mr. Connor said to take the rest of the day off. Sort of an early kick-off for the Fourth of July weekend. We can definitely go riding tomorrow."

"Yes!" Lilly smiled. "I almost forgot about the Fourth. What's there to do around here?"

"I don't know." Nate turned to Eric.

"Me either. It'll be my first year here, but I bet we can find out from the locals at the party tomorrow."

"It's a plan, then." Nate reached for Lilly's hand. "If you're ready, how about that riding lesson?"

"I'm ready."

"Lilly?" Eric interrupted.

"Yeah?"

"Think about what I said." He winked at her.

Nate's attention ping-ponged between her and Eric. Lilly tried to ignore it, but the heat rushed up her cheeks anyway. "Okay. See you tomorrow."

She pulled Nate down the path. When they passed between the two buildings, she let go and almost ran to the truck. *Please, don't let him ask questions.*

No such luck.

"What was that about?"

"Nothing." She tugged on the door, only to find it locked. With a sigh, she turned to watch him stalk up to within a foot of her location.

"Lilly?" Nate's brow furrowed in that glare she hadn't seen in a couple of days. "Was he flirting with you?"

"No! Why would you think that?"

"What do you need to think about, then?" His eyes bored into hers, pinning her against the truck.

"Nate Pierce, are you jealous?"

He stormed closer, pulling her into his arms and growling, "Hell, yeah."

Lilly didn't have time to respond before his lips came crashing down on hers. She was barely aware of her feet coming off the driveway as he lifted her up, or her back being pressed into the truck door as Nate leaned into her. Her arms gripped his shoulders. She instinctively wrapped her legs around him to keep from falling to the ground.

His firm lips nudged hers open. Everything screamed heat. Warm mouths, ragged gasping breaths. Sweat dripped down her back, between her breasts, and pooled behind her knees as their already hot bodies heated further. He smelled of dirt and sweat.

The only thing that mattered was his hands pressing her against his hard body, or his mouth moving down her neck, claiming her for his own. Because that was what he was doing. Staking a claim. The heat and demand of his kisses seared through her skin, branding her heart and soul. No one had ever kissed her like Nate Pierce.

She held on for dear life and kissed him back. She moved along his jawline, tasting the saltiness of his skin on her tongue. He groaned and moved to claim her lips again before she could try anything else.

All the days of built up anticipation sighed out of her body in the hiss of that smoking hot release, only to be replaced by a new tension. Lilly finally got her hands into his hair, knocking that stupid hat off his head. She didn't even care that it was damp with sweat. All she wanted was to pull him in tighter. Get as close as she could.

Nate's hands moved from her back, sliding along her side to grip her by the waist. Only the unbearably hot metal of the truck, his body, and her aching legs kept her from falling. His fingers kneaded her hips, sending little thrills shooting to places she hadn't been aware of in far too long. Her gasp broke his concentration. He stopped kissing her and rested his forehead on hers.

"Nate," she fought to catch her breath, "you don't have to be jealous."

Nate kissed her again. Softer this time. Teasing her, pulling on her lips with his teeth. "Oh?"

"No," she groaned against his lips. "You're the only one that's ever made me this hot."

"Ever?" he asked.

"Is that bad?"

"Maybe."

"Why?"

"It'd be easier if you'd felt this way with someone else."

"What do you mean?"

"Because I should walk away and let you be."

All the air rushed from her lungs. Lilly tried to untangle herself from Nate, but he kept her pressed between him and the truck, her legs dangling off the ground in an awkward way. "Let me down."

"No."

"No?"

"Not yet. Let me explain." Nate held her by her thighs, keeping them pressed together and her thoroughly turned on.

Lilly fidgeted until she realized that only made things worse. For both of them. "Nate, please."

He grinned.

She blushed. "Stop it."

"This might be the first time I've got you on the run." He chuckled, then got serious again. "I shouldn't have kissed you, but I'm tired of fighting this."

Lilly knew what he meant. "Me too."

"What do we do?"

She sighed. "Make a deal?"

His brow furrowed again. "What kind of deal?"

"No promises, and kisses only. For our safety."

"So, I can kiss you all I want?"

"Yes. But nothing else. Got it?"

"And you're okay with that?"

Lilly found it hard to breathe again. She looked into his stormy gray eyes. It was so easy to get lost in their mystery, but there were also depths of gentleness and acceptance she'd never felt in the other men she'd dated.

She traced down the side of his face, rough with afternoon stubble. "I don't know. I'm scared, you're scared. But if you don't agree to keep kissing me I'll have to go home to Texas. And remember, I'm not ready to go home."

"Is that so?" He bent close, smiling into her cheek, then nuzzling a sensitive spot near her ear. "Kissing is good."

He proceeded to kiss her face and neck until she feared she wouldn't be able to stand when he set her down. All she could do was hold on and enjoy the sensations. Each time she started to think it unfair he was doing all the exploring, he'd do something new and her mind would go blank. A nip on her earlobe had her moaning and digging her fingers into the base of his skull. That brought his lips back to her mouth.

"Nate." Lilly pulled away to gasp his name.

"Yes?"

"I need a cold shower."

He chuckled but let go of her legs. Lilly kept an iron hold on his arms so she didn't collapse right there in Eric Hunt's driveway .

"I'm gonna need one of these to get my keys." Nate nodded toward his right hand.

"Uh huh." She took a deep breath and let go.

~

*N*ate glanced at the clock again. Lilly said an hour. It had only been thirty minutes. Should he push his luck?

He smiled at the memory of dropping her off. She'd pointed at him and told him to stay in the truck. Then, with that fire he'd come to anticipate, she informed him if he showed up before an hour, she wouldn't be held responsible for her actions.

And he'd been tempted.

One kiss, and he'd been on fire. It was more than the years of abstinence. She'd fit perfectly in his arms, but that wasn't even all of it. She brought joy back into his life. He'd grown to respect her courage and enthusiasm for everything around her.

It had taken all he had to put her in the truck at Eric's and let her walk away at Mrs. Lilly's. In the end, it was the fear that helped him do it. And the guilt.

He'd always thought things were perfect with Mere. And they were. They'd had great chemistry, but it had been more of a slow comfortable burn.

Touching and kissing Lilly was more like a Michael Bay movie. All explosions and intense chase scenes. What did that mean? Could something like that last, or would it burn itself out?

He decided he'd take another cold shower before picking her up for her riding lesson.

When he finally got to Mrs. Lilly's, Nate's hands were sweating and his heart was racing with longing again. Now that he knew what she tasted like, keeping his distance would be harder than ever. He took several deep breaths before walking to her door. She answered seconds after he knocked.

"Hey." *Brilliant.* Nate cleared his throat. "Ready?"

"*Si.*" Lilly glanced up at him through her lashes then away quickly.

Nate liked it when she slipped into Spanish. He'd come to realize she did it when she was nervous or angry. She didn't look mad, so she must be as flustered as he was.

"Got your keys and phone?"

She rolled her eyes at him, and it helped break some of the tension. When they reached the truck, he only took her hand to help her in. It wasn't nearly as satisfying as holding her in his arms, but he knew they both needed the extra space. She gave him a grateful smile and squeeze of the hand before he closed her door.

"I forgot to tell you." Lilly had already adjusted her seat-belt so she could turn toward him. "I took your advice."

"Oh?"

"Last night I texted my mom and didn't call her Abby. It might still take a while, but you were right."

"Did she reply?"

"Not yet, but I already feel better." She touched her chest. "Like something finally broke loose. So, thank you."

Nate suspected the walls around his own heart crumbled when he glanced at her. He stretched his hand across the seat, and she laced her fingers with his. They sat in silence the rest of the short drive, both lost in their own thoughts. He was glad she was coming to terms with her situation, and he wondered if he had reached a place where he could change his. Maybe it was time to call his family. Not today, but soon.

He had to let her hand go to pull into Bear Mountain Stables. The parking lot was full of tourists since it was the middle of the day. It would make the initial lesson part less private, but once they got out on the trail, there was plenty of room to spread out.

"Wow, there are a lot of people here." Lilly took in all the cars. "Will we be able to ride?"

"Yep. Gyp is yours and no one else's."

"What about you?" She shielded her eyes to look up at him.

"I've got a horse too. His name is Blackberry."

"That's not a very manly name." She giggled and followed him toward the barn.

"Maybe not, but he's a good horse." Nate waved to one of the stable hands. "Hi, Michael. I'll be taking Gyp and Black-berry out for the afternoon. We'll head toward Lake Leatherwood."

"Sounds good. Should be a good ride today. Need your

water bottles filled?" Michael walked with them into the shade of the barn.

"Yes, please." Nate waved Lilly into a side room. "This is the tack room. All the saddles and other gear are stored here." He found his area and pulled his saddle bag out and retrieved two water bottles. After tossing them to Michael, he handed the bag to Lilly. "You carry this and I'll get the first saddle. After we get Blackberry ready, I'll teach you how to saddle Gyp."

"Okay."

They spent the next thirty minutes going step by step through the saddling process. First, Lilly watched while Nate did his own horse. Then he helped her saddle Gyp before he double checked everything.

Nate was glad that Mrs. Lilly's saddle was the right size for Lilly. It would have been harder to find one for her shorter legs without the special order one already at the stable.

"I'm not that short, Nate!" Lilly slapped his shoulder. "Stop teasing me."

"What are you? Three-four?" He grinned and helped her get her foot in the stirrup.

"I'm five-two." She settled in and waited while he mounted his horse. "Why is it such a big deal that you're more than a foot taller than me?"

"It's just fun to tease you." There was no way he'd admit it made him want to protect her. "All right, now let Gyp do her thing. She'll follow Blackberry and you won't have to worry about anything. It'll give you a chance to get used to being on a horse." Nate led Blackberry to his favorite trail, knowing Gyp would do just as he said. "Remember, let the reins rest loosely in your hands."

"Okay." Lilly sounded confident, and he had to admit, she looked it too.

"Are you sure you've never ridden before?"

"Like you said, Gypsy knows what's she's doing, and I trust her." She patted the horse's neck. "Isn't that right, girl?"

"You're a natural." Nate fell silent as they moved into the trees.

He knew exactly where he wanted to take Lilly. It was only half an hour ride through the woods to a corner of the lake. They could roll up their jeans and put their feet in the water, or just rest under the shade of the trees.

Nate couldn't remember the last time he'd taken a day off. The sun beat down on him, causing the sweat to roll, but the warm breeze brought the smells of summer—honeysuckle, grass, dust.

"Did you ride a lot when you were a veterinarian?" Lilly asked from behind.

"Yeah. I had my own horses, my own ranch, actually." That familiar longing, the homesickness lingered, but it wasn't as strong as it had been.

"Where was that?"

"Colorado."

"I've never been there, but I've seen pictures. It always looks pretty."

"It is. Of course, most places can be beautiful in their own way." Nate thought the hills and lakes of Arkansas were beautiful. Sometimes he missed the snow-capped mountains, but he'd grown used to this.

"That's true." Lilly was quiet a few minutes before she asked her next question. "Do you have family there?"

Nate squirmed in his seat, and Blackberry stiffened under him. He tried to relax, but he could feel Lilly's eyes on his back. Talking about his family was dangerous territory.

"Come on, Nate. You know about my family. Tell me something about yours. Do you have brothers or sisters?"

"No brothers. I do have a sister, but she ran away when

she was seventeen. We haven't heard from her in eight years."

Well, he hadn't heard from her.

"I'm sorry. Any idea why she ran away?"

"She felt trapped by the small town life. Said she wanted big cities, big opportunities." The bitterness leaked through his voice.

Natalie had been his opposite in every way. He'd never wanted to leave home, and yet he had too.

"Couldn't she have done that without cutting all ties with your family?" Lilly asked the one question he'd always fretted over.

The one point that had driven him crazy all these years. It wasn't chasing her dreams that had bothered him, but the way Nat had gone about it.

Lilly maneuvered Gypsy up beside Blackberry. "Hopefully, you'll find her."

"Whoa." Nate pulled back on his reins, grabbing Gyp's too. "Lilly, how would you feel if one of your family didn't talk to you for two years, then called you out of the blue?"

She didn't hesitate. "I'd be glad to hear from them. One time Gael couldn't call for three months because of a deployment. I can't describe how it felt to hear his voice after that long. Why do you ask?"

"Nat's not the only one who's maintained radio silence," he admitted. "I haven't been very communicative with my family, either."

Lilly looked away. When she turned back, there were tears in her eyes. "Why haven't you spoken to your parents?"

Nate reached out, and Lilly obliged him by offering her hand. This woman wore her emotions for everyone to see. Her concern for him was clear. He nudged Blackberry to sidestep closer to Gypsy. Once their sides were touching, he leaned over, pulling Lilly closer until he could kiss her cheek.

"Because I ran away too. But thanks to you, I think I'm

ready to face some of my fears. The first step is letting my family back in. Thank you for that." Nate moved from her cheek to her lips.

They were just as soft and inviting as the first time he'd kissed them. However, instead of the explosion of desire, this time was more of a steady flame. He found comfort in the fact their attraction wasn't all consuming, at least not all the time.

Gyp snorted and sidestepped, moving Lilly out of reach.

She laughed. "I guess Gypsy doesn't like sharing me."

"Come on, let's get to the lake, and I'll tell you more about my family."

~

*T*he water was beautiful. It reflected the blue sky, making the green of the trees that much greener. They tied the horses up, and Nate produced a blanket that he spread at the base of a tree.

"It'll be a little cooler in the shade." He sat and waved Lilly over. "Join me?"

She studied his face. He looked unsure. As if he thought she might ride off without him. It touched her that someone as handsome as him could be insecure. She sat down and leaned against the tree.

"Are you really going to tell me about your family?"

"I will if you tell me why it's so important for you to know." He too leaned back, their shoulders resting against each other.

"Because your family is a part of you. How else can I get to know you better?" She turned sideways and ran her fingers through the hair that lay across his forehead. It was thick, but soft between her fingers, not yet damp from the heat of the day. "I want to know what kind of boy you were. Did you drive your mother crazy? Did you help your dad?"

Nate reached up and took her hand in his. "What if I'd rather sit here and kiss you instead of talk?"

Lilly smiled. "I think we've kissed enough for a while. Tell me about your childhood. You can even stick to the good memories if that's easier."

"How do you know they're not all good memories?" He leaned close and kissed her so she couldn't answer his questions.

She sighed with pleasure, twining her fingers with his and letting him take the lead. He kept the kissing sweet, allowing her to keep her wits about her. However, it endeared him to her even more than the passionate kisses from earlier. These gentle explorations meant something.

When Nate finally pulled back, Lilly looked into his eyes. "Nate, it's time to stop running away. I know they're not all good memories because you're human." She placed both hands on either side of his face. Lilly kissed both cheeks, then his forehead. "And I can still see the pain in your eyes."

Nate's shoulders tensed.

"Nate." Lilly kissed his nose, then his lips briefly before continuing. "You don't have to tell me what hurt you, but let me help you remember what you loved about your family. At least for today."

For a moment, Nate's eyes widened. His gaze shifted all around as if he didn't want her to look at him, but he didn't jerk away. He finally exhaled.

"Okay."

"Good." Lilly tugged on his arms. "Lay down and close your eyes."

Nate obeyed, resting his head on her lap. Once he had shifted to a comfortable position, she massaged his face, forehead, and scalp until he was relaxed.

"You're going to put me to sleep," he murmured.

"Excuses, excuses." Lilly stopped the massage and just ran her fingers through his hair. "Tell me some of your favorite memories."

"My dad taught me to ride a horse when I was four. I don't remember a time when I couldn't ride. We always had horses. That's why the barn is my happy place, I think. The smell of horses, hay, saddle soap, even manure. It all reminds me of time with Dad."

She listened as he reminisced about the adventures they'd had on the ranch, enjoying the sound of his voice, the feel of his hair, and the way his face looked at the moment. He was calm, happy even, in his memories. The worry lines were gone, and with his eyes closed, so was the pain.

"What about your mom?"

"She loves to cook. We have a garden so everything is fresh in the summer." His lips turned up in a smile, and he opened his eyes. "You know, my mom's salsa could curl your toes."

"Oh yeah? We'll have to see about that." Lilly's fingers paused, the words leaving her mouth before she could think about them. She quickly resumed her trail through his hair, hoping he didn't think anything of her remark, and changed the subject. "Now tell me about your sister."

"Natalie was always getting into trouble. Not on purpose. She just had to learn everything the hard way."

"But you accepted what your parents told you?"

"More or less." He chuckled. "Nat wasn't a bad girl. She just wanted more than the ranch life offered."

"Have you tried to find her?" Lilly's heart ached for him, for his parents. She didn't know if she could stand it if one of her siblings disappeared. That was part of what made it so hard to know her mom had kept her grandma a secret all their lives.

"Yeah, but we haven't had much luck. I'll admit I haven't done much since moving here. I figure she'll come home when she's ready. Kind of like me, I guess."

Lilly nodded, but an uneasy feeling settled in her chest. "Nate, what if she needs help? Don't give up on her."

Nate sat up and pulled her close. "I won't."

FRIDAY

*T*hey decided not to go riding the day of the party. Instead, Nate took care of some errands around town while Lilly spent the morning going through boxes. After lunch, she used the fresh produce Nate dropped off to make a batch of homemade salsa. She added extra peppers, hoping to give Nate's mom's salsa a run for her money.

The day dragged. Everything she did brought Nate to mind.

Lilly laughed when he arrived early so they could sit and kiss before the party. He made the "kissing only" rule unbearably hard, but she knew if she crossed that line, she might never recover her heart.

It was almost a relief to let Nate set her in his truck and head to town and chaperones. Eric's driveway and the surrounding section of Spring Street were crowded with cars and trucks. Tiki torches lined a path to the backyard, where fairy lights had been strung around the borders. More torches and some Chinese lanterns finished the lighting. The area felt even smaller with the crowd of people mingling there.

Lilly walked hand in hand with Nate in spite of the warm night. Their hands were sweaty, but she didn't care. She wanted to hold onto whatever this was as long as she could. She carried her salsa in her other hand, and he carried the bag of chips.

Nate gazed down at her. "You okay?"

She nodded. "Are you okay with this?" She lifted their hands.

He kissed her knuckles before letting their hands drop back to their sides. A warmth that didn't have anything to do with the summer air moved through her body.

"Lilly!" Flo ran over and gave her a side hug. "I haven't seen you for days. How's everything?"

"I've been busy helping Nate with this project, but it's great." Lilly hugged her back.

Flo winked at Nate. "I see."

"Don't act so surprised. I'm sure this is what you and Roberta have been scheming about all along." Nate reclaimed Lilly's hand.

Flo just wagged a finger his direction and laughed. "Go on and find the younger people." She disappeared into the crowd.

"Do you know everyone?" Lilly asked.

"Most." He shrugged but didn't move to talk to any of them.

"But you don't hang out with any of them?"

"Not really."

Lilly squeezed his hand. "Why not?"

"People ask questions."

"Okay, then I won't ask, even if I want to." And she wanted to. "Hey, there's Kerri's friend Jennifer."

"You have a good memory."

It was a familiar face, at least. Lilly tugged him that direction. Jennifer stood by a man in khaki shorts and a gray polo shirt. His dark blond hair was brushed back in an almost spiky style, but more subdued than punk, and his blue eyes were focused solely on Kerri's friend. He looked pleasantly engaged. The woman, on the other hand, looked agitated.

"I'm a good teacher and an even better coach. You're making a judgment call based on your ego." She crossed her arms over her chest. "It's not professional."

"You're too emotional to be a good role model for the girls." The guy's voice was calm, but Lilly swore there was a glimmer of something in his eyes. She just didn't know if it was malice or humor.

"Girls are emotional. Always. They'll trust me because they'll know I understand what they're going through. It's what they need in a mentor." Jennifer threw her arms up in the air and waved them around. "Are you trying to be difficult? Do you have better candidates?"

"I can't discuss other applicants with you." He shook his head, then his eyes landed on Nate and Lilly. He held his hand out. "Hi, I'm Robert Allen, principal at the high school."

Nate took the hand. "Nate Pierce, with Connor Landscaping. This is Lilly Ramirez."

"Hey, it was Jennifer, right?" Lilly ignored Robert, instinctively moving to the woman's side. "How are you?"

"Oh, hi. I'm fine, and my friends call me Jen." Jen's shoulders were tight, but she shrugged, and they relaxed a little. "Sorry. I interviewed for the women's track coach position today, and Mr. Allen isn't going to hire me."

"Oh?" Lilly turned to the principal.

"I didn't say I wouldn't hire her, just that I have concerns." He scanned the crowd. "This isn't the place to talk about it."

"You may not think so, but I'm running out of time to find a job close to home." Jen scowled at the man.

"Jen," Robert started but she cut him off.

"It's Jennifer." She returned to the arms-crossed position.

"But you just said—" Robert's eyes widened for a fraction of a second before he crossed his own arms and indulged her with a staring match.

"I'm being professional. We're not friends, Mr. Allen."

"In that case, it's Dr. Allen."

Nate coughed, and Lilly was pretty sure it was to hide a laugh. She felt sorry for Jen, but arguing probably wasn't the best way to get the job.

Lilly looked for a new topic of conversation. "Have you seen Kerri?"

"Eric dragged her over by the pond." Jen pointed just as someone rang a cowbell to get everyone's attention.

The crowd grew quiet and turned as one toward the back corner where the sound of the waterfall marked the little pond.

Lilly couldn't see over the people in front of her. She shifted from foot to foot, but no matter how she moved, she couldn't get a good view of Eric and Kerri.

"What's happening?" she whispered to Nate.

"Looks like Eric's—" He cut himself off when Eric started talking.

"Kerri, five months ago I came to Eureka Springs to find myself. I was disillusioned with my abilities as an artist and afraid that everyone around me only wanted to ride the coattails of my fame and fortune. I was in danger of becoming lost and bitter. Then I stumbled into your shop." Eric paused.

Lilly tried again to see around the people in front of her. She resorted to watching the others around her for their reactions. Jen's hand flew up to her mouth, the smile barely hidden. The breeze shifted, and smoke from the grill wafted over them.

Eric continued, "These last few months have been better

than the last several years combined. You've helped me laugh again. Every day I wake up and can't wait to see you, to be with you. All I care about is making you happy. Please, let me do that. Say you'll marry me."

The silence was deafening. No one breathed. Only the crickets dared chirp.

Since Lilly couldn't see Kerri, she listened and waited for the happy reaction. It didn't come. Nate's brow furrowed. Jen's smile dissolved. The principal watched Jen.

"You deserve more than I can give," Kerri said, her voice finally breaking through the crowd.

There was a collective gasp. Lilly grabbed Nate's arm and climbed up on the rock border of the garden in an effort to see something. Kerri pushed her way past them, away from Eric, away from what should have been a joyful moment.

Jen scanned the crowd and yelled, "Jaya, Brynn!"

"Behind you, go!" The black woman from the church shoved her way toward them, followed by a brunette and a blonde man with floppy hair. All four chased after Kerri, disappearing around the corner of the house.

"Wait here." Nate spoke close to her ear, then pulled free from her grasp.

Lilly's heart raced. *What was going on?* "Nate?"

She turned in a circle, but he was gone. Not knowing what else to do, she obeyed. Lilly clutched the bowl of salsa that had never made it to the table and stared at the principal.

Robert nodded at the disappearing group. "Any insight into what's happened?"

Lilly shook her head. "No. Eric clearly adores Kerri, and every time I see them together, it's obvious she's head over heels for him."

"Sometimes it's all in the timing." Robert shrugged and

looked off in the direction Kerri, Jen, and the others had gone.

"Maybe." Lilly didn't know why Kerri would be insecure in her relationship. What did timing matter with love?

"Well, guess I'll call it a night." Robert waved goodbye and made his way through the crowd.

Alone and confused, Lilly searched for Nate. Kerri's quick departure had left a cloud over the gathering. Everyone seemed to know those two should be together. Why couldn't Kerri see it? Lilly's heart ached for her new friend. What was going on? Why would she say no to a man that looked at her the way Eric did? Lilly would give anything for that kind of love.

Where was Nate? She turned again, heart pounding, hating that she didn't want to be alone.

"Lilly?" Nate appeared beside her, placing a hand on the small of her back. "Ready to go?"

The warmth of that hand, the steadiness of his presence, calmed her. She sank into him. "Yes. Did you see Eric? Is he okay? What about Kerri?"

"We can talk in the truck." He guided her to the front and down the road. Most people drifted to their vehicles. Nate pointed toward the retreating crowd. "Sure you don't want to join them in town?"

"Definitely not." Lilly grabbed his hand and pulled them into a run, the bowl of salsa cradled like a football, determined to get to his truck as fast as possible.

"What's the rush?" Nate's characteristic chuckle signified he might have a clue what she was thinking. "Do you need answers that badly?"

"No."

As soon as they reached the truck, she set the salsa on the floor and climbed in without letting his hand go. Then she tugged him close, wrapped her arms around his neck, and pulled him down so she could reach his lips.

Some of Lilly's confusion over Kerri running from everything Lilly had ever wanted leaked out in the desperation of that kiss. How long until whatever this was with Nate disappeared?

Nate answered with tenderness, slowing her frenzied attempts to push him further.

He untangled her hands from around his neck. "Come on, you still need to eat."

"Why are you always trying to feed me?" she pouted.

"Because someone has to watch out for you."

Lilly sighed and leaned back in her seat while Nate walked around to his side. She'd always wanted someone to watch out for her. Papi did the best he could with Mama pushing and prodding right through every potential tender moment.

Even though she loved her older brother and sister, they'd always been too busy with their own lives. She was closest to Gael and Selena, her younger siblings. They did pretty well watching out for each other growing up, but now they were scattered all over the world.

Nate climbed into the truck. "What do you feel like?"

"Surprise me?" She liked that he'd already surprised her in so many ways. "Nate, there was a woman who left with Jen. She was at church too."

"What did she look like?"

"Black, really pretty, kind of sad eyes."

"That's Jaya." He turned out of town. "How about I cook something for you?"

"That sounds wonderful." Lilly shifted in her seat. "Tell me about Jaya."

"I've only talked with her a few times. Mostly when

helping with the memorial to her fiancé Aiden. He died really late Valentine's night in a car accident."

"How sad!"

Nate nodded but didn't say anything else. He gripped the steering wheel tightly, his lips pressed in a white line, and Lilly wondered where his thoughts had gone.

SATURDAY

*L*illy chose one of her grandma's vintage red dresses with white polka dots to wear to town for the Fourth of July activities. She left her hair in waves around her shoulders but tucked a hair-tie in her purse in case the heat became unbearable and she needed it off her neck.

Nate picked her up early enough for them to get downtown in time for all the morning events. She wasn't sure what to expect, but it would be better than sitting at home.

They hovered on the edge of a small crowd near the auditorium where apple pies were being judged. It looked like all three Hanes sisters had entered. They wore matching T-shirts with sequined American flags on them, headbands with sparkling stars that bobbed above their heads, and red white and blue tutus. It looked like the judges had separated them from each other with the other contestants so they couldn't bicker among themselves.

Lilly liked the way so many from town knew each other and interacted with a familiar camaraderie. She could tell who were tourists. They hung around the edges like her and Nate.

She glanced up at him. He didn't look uncomfortable. In fact, he gazed at the scene with what could be called fondness. His isolation was a choice, not a disposition.

"Hey, Nate." A guy in board shorts with rumpled blond hair and blue eyes walked toward them.

The brunette next to him was dressed to kill in a simple short romper paired with wedge heels and perfectly manicured nails. If it weren't for the linked hands, she wouldn't have picked them out as a couple. They were complete opposites. It took a moment for Lilly to recognize them as the couple who'd followed Jen and Kerri the night before.

"Mic, Brynn." Nate greeted them with a nod, then focused on the man. "How's Eric?"

Lilly tried to listen in on the conversation, but the woman stretched out her hand.

"Hi, I'm Brynn."

"Lilly Ramirez. Are you friends with Kerri?"

"All my life. Love the dress. Where did you get it?"

"It was my grandmother's."

"Of course. You can't buy quality like that anymore. The colors are still so vibrant. It looks wonderful on you too."

"Thanks." Lilly was surprised at the genuine compliment from a woman so obviously put together. It gave her courage to ask her own question. "I've been worried about Kerri. She's been so nice to me since I came to Eureka Springs. Will she be okay?"

It was fascinating to watch Brynn's perfect porcelain features softened in concern. "She's scared. Her arthritis is getting worse, and she doesn't want Eric to be stuck with that. Eric loves her, though. She'll figure it out."

Lilly felt a stupid lump clog her throat. She barely knew these people, but she felt connected to them all. "Thanks. If there's something I can do, will you let me know?"

Brynn nodded. "Sure."

Nate's hand rested on Lilly's lower back, and she leaned into it, grateful for that contact.

"Looks like they've chosen a winning pie." His voice rumbled near her ear, successfully distracting her. "It's one of the Hane's sisters. Melissa, maybe?"

Mic laughed, stepping to Brynn's side. "Good guess, but that one's Margaret."

Nate laughed too. "What's next?"

"They'll crown a Ms. Apple Pie and a Mr. Firecracker before the parade starts. It'll wind up the street, then there'll be a watermelon seed spitting contest back here." Brynn's smile was award-winning.

Lilly couldn't help but smile along with her. "It sounds like fun."

"It doesn't take long. Then there isn't much until the fireworks tonight out on Beaver Lake. Are you guys going?" Brynn asked.

Nate glanced at Lilly, and she stared back before shrugging. "We didn't really know what there was to do around here."

"Mic has a boat. You should join us. Kerri and Eric are coming as well as Jen and Jaya." Brynn latched onto Mic's arm. "There's plenty of room, and it's a great show."

"You should come." Mic confirmed the invitation.

"What do you think, Lilly?" Nate's gaze let her know it was entirely up to her.

Before she could answer, Brynn added, "Bring your swimsuits. We always go early and swim beforehand."

Nate swallowed hard, and Lilly burst out laughing.

Nate grumbled, "They're all trying to kill me."

"Nate Pierce, you can't swim?" Lilly teased him.

"Very funny." Nate tapped Lilly's nose, then turned to Mic. "We'd love to come. Where and what time?"

"Meet us at the visitor's center at six. You can follow us out from there."

"Thanks, Mic." Nate waved and turned to go.

Lilly held him up. "Um, Brynn?"

"Yeah?"

"Know a good place I could get a swimsuit?"

Brynn looked her over. "You're closest to Kerri's size. I'll have her bring an extra, so no worries."

"Thanks. See you later." Lilly waved and let Nate lead her away.

"What would you have done if you couldn't find a suit?" Nate asked.

"Wouldn't you like to know?" She grinned up at him and kept walking. He grabbed her by the waist and swung her off her feet. "Nate Pierce, you put me down."

"Not until you tell me what you would have done." He turned her around until she faced him, her body pressed up against his and her feet dangling off the ground.

Lilly wrapped her arms around his neck and barely restrained herself from clinging to him with her legs too. Instead, she left them hanging awkwardly while he kept a tight grip on her hips.

"What is it with you keeping me hanging in the air?"

"Maybe I like you here." He nuzzled her neck.

"You're awful." She laughed unconvincingly.

"Just answer the question."

"I would have worn a matching bra and panty set. They don't look any different than bikinis anyway." She stared him in the eye, determined not to tell him she hated bikinis. They left her feeling exposed and uncomfortable.

In truth, she would have worn cutoffs and a tank to swim in, but she liked the way he looked at her. Like he wanted to get her alone and all to himself.

"We should take the horses out for another ride today." He whispered against her mouth.

Oh yeah. She could do with a few hours alone with this man. Outside would be safe.

A couple of hours later she wasn't so sure how safe the outdoors were. They had taken a short ride to a small valley shaded with large trees. Nate spread a blanket out for them. It was too hot to snuggle, thank goodness, but the man could still do serious damage with his kisses.

He was working his way down her neck when he murmured, "Do they match right now?"

"Do what match?" She could barely think.

"Your bra and panties?"

"No." She sighed.

"Probably for the best."

She nodded but didn't mean it. It was so hot. If only she were the reckless type. "Nate?"

"Mmhmm?" he worked his way along her chin to her ear.

"You should know, I don't usually make out like this. I mean, we haven't even been on a date." She gasped as he sucked on her earlobe.

"I've taken you out to eat a couple times."

Lilly laughed. "And we know how well that turned out."

He moved back to the nape of her neck. "It looks pretty good from where I'm at."

The distance between their bodies was starting to frustrate her. She pushed him down to the blanket, hooking one leg over his body and half draping herself over him. Gazing into his eyes, she traced the contours of his face with her fingers.

"What are we doing, Nate?"

"I like when you say my name all breathy like that." He pulled her in for another kiss. When he released her, he answered her question. "We're exploring."

"Okay." But was it? What happened when it was time for her to go back to Dallas?

Nate kissed her again and rational thought turned fuzzy once more.

~

*M*ic's boat was a twenty-foot pontoon that looked to be a hundred years old. Nate scowled and wondered if it was seaworthy. He'd followed Mic down the pier while Lilly went to the bathroom with Kerri. Eric had stepped into the bait shop for ice and drinks.

Mic slapped him on the back as if reading his thoughts, "I promise she floats. Old man Peterson sold her to me a couple of weeks ago, and I had the bottom resurfaced. She's got a good engine on her too."

Brynn was right beside him. "You should consider remodeling the entire thing. Maybe put in a cabin for changing as well."

"I don't think we need a cabin."

"But we could come out with our friends more often if we made it nicer."

"Brynn." Mic shot her a look Nate would have interpreted as a 'let's talk about this later look,' but it didn't appear as if that's how Brynn took it. She opened her mouth to say something else, but Mic pulled her in and kissed her instead.

"Well, I guess that's one way to win an argument with Brynn." Jaya joined them on the pier. She carried a large beach bag and towel. "Hey, Nate. Kerri and Lilly will be back in a minute."

"I haven't seen you since the memorial. How are you doing?"

She shrugged. "Okay. Working, trying to keep busy."

Nate nodded. That was the only way to survive. He

thought about telling Jaya that, but then he'd have to admit to understanding her situation.

Lilly and Kerri walked toward them, Eric close behind pulling a wagon full of supplies. Lilly wore the same clothes she'd had on earlier, so he could only assume she now wore swimwear underneath the t-shirt and shorts.

"Yay, we're all here. Let's get this party started!" Brynn danced to the console and flicked the key to turn on the radio while everyone stowed supplies and found seats.

"What about Jen?" Jaya asked.

"She bailed on us. Something about a bike race today." Brynn moved so Mic could sit and start the engine. "Jeremy invited her to cheer him on."

"I didn't think she liked Jeremy." Kerri spread a towel on a seat.

"She doesn't," Jaya replied. "He just doesn't take no for an answer."

"He's going to take this as encouragement," Kerri sighed. "She'll need chocolate for sure tomorrow."

The conversation drifted around them as Lilly stepped beside Nate, her hand brushing his. He wanted to lace his fingers through hers but didn't. They'd agreed on no kissing where others could see. That had been a stupid idea. Especially when she smiled up at him like that.

"Now you're just teasing me," he whispered.

"I'd never do that." She took his hand and led him to a seat. "Maybe Brynn can find a Latin music channel?"

"Heaven help me if she does."

Lilly laughed. It didn't take long until Mic had them cruising across the lake toward the fireworks site. The plan was to stop somewhere halfway to swim and jump off some cliffs before going the rest of the way to pile in with the other boats to watch the show.

"Sorry, I don't have any tubes to pull yet." Mic steered while Brynn sat beside him.

"No big deal." Eric sat with Kerri nestled next to him.

No one had mentioned the party from the night before, and Kerri and Eric acted like they were still a couple. There was a little awkward tension, but it seemed like they were going on as usual.

Jaya had a scarf tied around her hair and big sunglasses. She'd been quiet most of the trip, carefully avoiding looking at the couples on board. Nate knew it must be strange for her to be the odd one out since Jen hadn't come. Brynn kept trying to draw Jaya into conversations with little luck.

Jaya talked the most with Lilly, who seemed to have a talent for drawing people out of themselves with her enthusiasm. Nate sat back and listened to Jaya go on about the rock formations around the lake. It wasn't until Jaya talked about the plants and ecosystem that Lilly was able to do more than just give Jaya her attention.

His heart warmed while he watched the two of them. Maybe Lilly was what all the broken people of Eureka Springs needed. She was good at listening and making you feel cared about again.

"There it is." Mic pointed toward shore where lots of people were jumping from the rocks. "That's a good spot to swim, and the more adventuresome can jump off those ledges. They're not too tall, but the water is deep so it's safe."

"Doesn't sound like you have to be too adventurous then." Nate shielded his eyes for a better look. The cliff face looked about ten feet high.

"It feels higher when you're standing on top." Mic turned them inland, cutting the engines about twenty feet from shore. "Anyone volunteering to stay on board to keep the boat from floating away or bumping another boat?"

"I'll stay." Jaya waved at him. "You go have fun."

"I'll hang out with Jaya. Cliff jumping was never my thing." Brynn pulled out a bottle of tanning lotion. "I'll work on my tan instead."

"Okay, yell if you need me." Mic kissed Brynn's nose before peeling his shirt off and diving in the water.

"That was quick." Lilly held the rail as the boat rocked.

Kerri and Eric ditched their outerwear a little slower than Mic but were already heading to the foot of the boat to jump in.

"Do you want to swim, or hang out here?" Nate held his breath, unsure if he could handle Lilly in a two-piece swimsuit. There was hope though. Kerri currently wore a one piece, so he might survive the day.

"I want to jump." She hooked her thumb over her shoulder toward the cliff.

"Really?"

"Yep."

She stood and pulled the t-shirt over her head revealing the top of a solid black swim-top with a v-neckline. It wasn't indecent, but it highlighted her assets nicely. Her skin looked smooth, begging him to touch. He swallowed as she shimmied out of the cut-offs.

Yep. Her legs were perfection. Every. Single. Inch.

"Nate." Lilly snapped her fingers in his face. "I take it you're a leg guy."

"I'm." He dragged his eyes to her face. "Um. Yeah."

"Then thank you."

"Well, I'm offended. You didn't even look at our legs." Brynn sat next to Jaya and posed. "What do you think of ours?"

"Um." Nate wanted to crawl in a hole. Jaya wouldn't look at him, but Brynn grinned like the Cheshire Cat. "They're nice. Really nice."

Brynn laughed and Lilly joined her. Jaya smiled but still didn't say anything.

Lilly tugged on his arm. "Come on, Nate Pierce. I'm a shoulders and abs girl. Let's see what you've got."

"Yes! Give us a show mower boy." Brynn slid her sunglasses to the top of her head.

Nate squirmed.

"Nate," Lilly whispered, drawing his attention back to her. "Look right here." She pointed to herself and quirked one brow up at him.

"Yes, ma'am." He grabbed the edge of his shirt and slowly pulled it over his head, ignoring the other two women. Instead, he focused on Lilly, getting a heady thrill out of knowing she watched him undress. Her eyes moved from his collarbone, past his pectorals, down his abs. A little smile teased the corner of her lips. "Well?"

"You'll do." She turned, climbed up on the bench, and jumped over the side of the boat with a whoop.

He barely registered the wolf whistle from Brynn as he climbed the edge of the boat.

"Why you little," he watched her surface before following her into the water.

She swam with sure easy strokes, but his longer ones brought him alongside her quickly. He wrapped one arm around her waist, tangling his legs with hers as he pulled her in close.

Their legs kept bumping into each other as they kicked to stay afloat while clinging to one another. They were close enough Nate could feel her chest rise and fall with each breath.

"I'll do?" he bent close. "What'll I do for?"

"Nate, they'll see," she sounded breathless.

He liked her breathless. Water dripped from her lashes, from her lips.

"Maybe I don't care." He leaned in.

She rested a finger on his lips. "Wait until dark."

"Why?"

"Because we both know I can't stay."

He crushed her against him, feeling the loss even though it hadn't happened yet.

Nate took a deep breath and relaxed his grip. She was right. Lilly would leave. Maybe not the way Meredith had, but she would leave. He needed to remember that. After tonight, he needed to put more space between them, but he wanted to enjoy today.

"Okay, but I want a kiss under the fireworks."

"Me too." Her smile melted his heart. "Now, race me to shore?"

"Okay." He gave her a mighty push in the right direction, enjoying her shriek of laughter. "Go!"

He matched his stroke to hers so they arrived at the same time.

"You didn't even try," she chastised him while splashing water in his direction.

"Sure I did. I tried very hard to let you win. It's not my fault you couldn't capitalize on that."

That brought another onslaught of water pushed in his general direction. "Nate Pierce!"

He jumped through her attack and pulled her down into the water with him. She squirmed and wiggled, bringing her body into full contact with his when she clung to him until he lifted them both to the surface. Her hands were clasped behind his neck, bringing her face closer to his.

Before she let him go, she whispered, "You're perfect."

Her eyes went wide before dropped into the lake with a splash and came up sputtering. Nate watched her retreat to climb up the rocks to a little path that led up the side of the hill. Eric and Kerri were waiting up there with Mic and several other people.

Lilly didn't look back. Had she meant to say those words? He knew he wasn't perfect, and he knew she knew it too. What had she meant then?

He watched those flawless legs climb over the rough terrain. Lilly was a lot like her legs. Beautiful and strong. Capable of doing hard things and looking great while doing it.

"Are you coming, Nate?" Eric yelled from above.

They were looking down at him while he stared at Lilly. Great. So much for keeping things secret.

"Yep." He hurried after the woman he couldn't stop thinking about.

Mrs. Lilly, Mere? What should I do? He didn't expect an answer, but he desperately needed one.

Most of the strangers had jumped by the time he reached the summit. Mic was right. It looked higher from above than it had from below. Lilly inched to the edge to peek over. His instinct was to hold onto her, to keep her from falling.

"Wow. Okay, Mic. Tell us how it's done." Lilly squared off with the ledge.

Mic pointed straight in front of him. "Take a good jump that way and land feet first. Watch."

Lilly stepped back. Mic retreated three steps then rushed the edge and leaped. He yelled as he flew a few feet before sailing into the water below. Nate's stomach dropped just watching. He glanced at Eric and saw the same look of concern mirrored in his eyes.

Kerri pulled her hand free from her boyfriend's grip, kissed him on the cheek, and said, "See you below."

Then she too jumped, leaving the three newbies standing up top. Eric exhaled when Kerri surfaced and waved at him.

"Can't be that bad." Lilly bent over the side for a better view.

Nate needed to pull her away from the edge. "We don't have to jump if you don't—"

Before he could reach for her, Lilly leaped and fell screaming all the way to the water. His heart pounded against his ribcage, and he sucked in a deep breath when her head popped up below.

"Scared the crap out of you didn't it?" Eric murmured.

"Yeah." He barely restrained himself from clutching his chest in an effort to slow down his heart.

"You realize we can't let our girls outdo us."

"Aw, hell." Nate's stomach dropped to his feet.

"On three?"

"Three!" Nate yelled, and they both jumped.

The cliff jumping got easier the more they did it, but he still held his breath until Lilly surfaced each time. She was fearless.

Nate found it best to jump with her. That way he was there as soon as she took that first breath after hitting the water. Knowing he would be close if she needed him calm edhim. But she didn't need him.

Eventually, they returned to the boat where they had gourmet snacks thanks to Mic and Kerri's passion for food before journeying to another spot to watch the fireworks.

The sunset on the lake was beautiful in spite of the hundreds of boats cluttering the waterway. Nate claimed a seat in a corner and Lilly settled in next to him. The cool breeze made sitting close bearable in the summer heat. It wasn't dark, but Nate placed his arm around her, letting his hand trace up and down her soft skin. She shivered and shifted closer.

The other couples had snuggled in for the show too. Only Jaya sat alone at the front of the boat, her feet dangling off the front. She reminded him of how solitary he'd been only weeks ago. Surrounded by people, but detached just the same. He bent down to rest his chin in the crook where Lilly's neck and shoulder met. Was it wrong to want to be with someone again?

He breathed her in, enjoying her warmth and goodness.

She sighed into him. "What are you thinking about?"

Nate searched for an appropriate and safe answer. "Nothing. Everything. Wondering what my family's doing tonight."

"Have you talked to them?"

"Not yet."

She turned to face him, taking his face in both her hands. "Nate, you have to call them."

"I will."

"When?"

"Tomorrow."

"Promise?"

Something in her eyes tugged at his heart. Why was it so important to her that he talk to his family?

"I promise." He nodded and rested his hands on hers.

The relief in her expression was immediate. She leaned in and gave him a quick peck on the lips. A barely there kiss, but the tenderness behind it spoke volumes. "You won't regret it."

She turned back as the first rocket shot into the sky. The red and blue colors bursting to life. Nate held her tight and kissed below her ear. He wouldn't regret a moment spent with her either.

SUNDAY

*N*ate hadn't planned on spending Sunday with Lilly, but he woke up thinking about her and couldn't stay away. He knew she'd be at church. After arguing with himself all morning, he walked in late. Luckily, there had been a seat right beside Lilly at the back.

He couldn't remember a word the preacher said. All he knew was Lilly smelled like summer sitting beside him— coconut and honeysuckle. It was a strange mixture of beach and southern roads, but it worked. He'd been aware of her thigh next to his, her shoulder tucked up beside him.

"Nate?" She was staring up at him with those lovely caramel eyes.

"Yes?"

"It's over."

Nate wasn't ready to say goodbye, but he knew he shouldn't press his luck and be alone with the woman who had become an obsession for him.

However, he wanted one more day to pretend she could be his. "How about we walk down the street?"

"That sounds wonderful."

It was warm out, but the humidity had dropped, making it bearable for the time being. They walked hand in hand, not even talking. Every once in a while, Nate would glance at Lilly and she would smile up at him.

A band was setting up in Basin Park so they found a spot in the shade to sit and listen.

"What do you think they're going to play?" Lilly's eyes twinkled with mischief.

"Why do you ask?"

"Cause I feel like dancing."

"Something tells me you always feel like dancing."

"Just when you're around." She winked at him.

"Hey, you said kissing only. No dancing." He teased her back.

The band started with a lively blues tune. Lilly tapped her foot for a couple of minutes before jumping up.

"You don't have to dance with me, but if there's music I can't sit still."

She was so full of life. Other people got up and danced. Kids laughed and ran around. Lilly moved and swayed and he was captivated. Nate wanted to join her, but it wasn't who he was.

Lilly danced closer and held out her hands. "Come on, Nate."

He surveyed the area, but it didn't look like anyone was watching him so he stood awkwardly on the sidelines of the park.

"Don't worry about what anyone else thinks." Lilly moved their hands with the music. "Just let the music in. Let it move you."

She kept their arms moving until he did something with his legs. It was more of a shuffle than a dance step, but it was enough for her to beam at him like he'd just won some contest on TV. His heart was hers at that moment.

"Now, like this." She moved his hands to her waist and placed hers on his hips, gently moving them to the rhythm.

Every coherent thought left his mind. He could only think of her hands pressing into him, moving him where she wanted. Her face tilted up to gaze at him, her eyes locked with his.

"Lilly." He didn't even know what to say.

"Mm-hmm?" She stepped closer.

"I can't dance."

Lilly swiveled her hips in time with his as she moved closer. Her eyes twinkling up at him.

"You're doing just fine."

Hours later, Nate dropped Lilly off at home. She stood on tiptoe and kissed him. It was one of those slow, sweet tortures that had him wishing the night would never end, but she pulled away too soon.

"Go home. Call your parents."

"Okay." He rested his chin on the top of her head.

"Promise me, Nate."

"I promise." He breathed her in, reluctant to let her go, knowing he couldn't risk everything again. No matter how much he wanted to.

"Good." She backed away and unlocked the door. "See you soon."

He didn't say goodbye. He couldn't.

When he got home, he called his parents before he could talk himself out of it. Lilly had been right. They were so happy to hear from him that they hadn't been angry or disappointed.

Nate talked to his parents for over an hour about everything that had changed over the last two years. They still had the ranch but wanted him to take it over so they could retire to Florida like they planned. Nate knew he wasn't ready for that. They said they understood.

He told them about Lilly, how she helped him remember what was important.

"She sounds smart, Nathaniel." His mom always called him by his full name. "If she's helping you move on, she must be very special."

"When will we get to meet her son?" his dad asked.

"I don't know. We're just friends. She's from Texas and all." He couldn't even admit to them he wasn't going to see her again. It didn't bode well for his commitment to that fact.

His parents fired off a hundred other questions, none of which he knew the answers to. He was grateful and confused at the hurt he felt that they didn't mention Meredith or the baby he'd lost. If he was moving on, why did the pain keep coming back?

Because you haven't told her about us. Meredith's voice whispered into his heart like a dagger.

He'd done everything in his power to keep his wife and child a secret from Lilly. He wasn't sure why, but he was scared that sharing them would mean they were really gone. That he was letting go, and he shouldn't have to let them go.

"Nate?" his dad asked again.

"What was that?" Nate tried to focus on the conversation.

"When will you come home?"

"I'm not sure, but I'll let you know. There are some things I need to figure out first." Nate rubbed the back of his neck.

"But it's been two years." His mom came back on the line. "I thought that's what you've been doing all this time."

"No mom, I've been hiding. Now, I'm figuring."

There was a moment of silence, then his dad finally said, "Well, I'm glad, son. Really glad. Take your time. You're moving in the right direction, just keep us in the loop. We love you."

"Thanks, dad."

WEDNESDAY

*I*t had been three days since Nate had seen Lilly. They'd been torture, but necessary. Each day proved Lilly had become too important for him to just give her up. One moment he thought he could go to her, but the next he'd let the fear of losing her like Meredith fill him with terror.

The weekend had been wonderful. He'd enjoyed every touch, every kiss. They'd laughed and talked, and he'd even had fun with the group out on the lake. It had been forever since he'd done anything social like that and not felt like an outsider looking in. Lilly made him happy. She made him a better person.

Was it worth the risk?

By Wednesday night Nate couldn't stay away from her any longer. He'd spent long hours at work, all of them filled with thoughts of her. What was she doing? When was she leaving? Would she find him before she left?

And the question that mattered more than any of them, could he let her go?

He decided to go see her and hope he'd know what to do.

God? Mrs. Lilly, Mere? Let me know what's best for her.

Lilly was outside working in the little flower bed when he arrived at the house, once more in cutoffs and smudged with dirt. Nate thought she was the cutest thing he'd ever seen. All woman, and yet sweet girl at the same time. He didn't understand how she pulled it off.

"Nate." She stood and brushed her hands off. "I was starting to think you were done with me."

That one phrase had him pulling her off her feet to prove how untrue that statement was. He loved how quickly her lips parted to welcome him in. Her fingers kneaded the base of his neck and her tongue darted in to parry with his. She pressed herself closer and he felt the thrum of blood through his veins moving quickly toward the danger zone.

"I'm afraid I'll never be done with you. That's why I tried to stay away." He rested his chin on the top of her head, thinking it would allow him to calm down.

Unfortunately, Lilly used that as an opportunity to nuzzle her way inside his neckline where she pressed a kiss to his Adam's apple. Her hands slid under his shirt against his skin, sending waves of fire skittering across his sides. Then she nipped the lower edge of his collarbone at the base of his neck.

She pushed him backward, into the shade of the porch until the back of his legs hit the rocking chair. He sat and she straddled him, never breaking the kiss.

"Holy hell." Nate pulled back to catch his breath. "Gotta slow down."

Lilly breathed as heavy as he did. She rested her face in the crook of his neck. Each puff of breath fanning the flames higher.

"Really, have to slow down or this will go too far real quick." He tried to move her off his lap, but she clung to him.

"Then give me something to remember when I leave. I've

never felt like this, and I doubt I ever will again." She burrowed into him again.

Nate groaned. "You have no idea how much I'd like that, but it wouldn't be right. Not like this."

She finally pulled back, giving him a little room to breathe. "Why not, Nate? I'm not asking you for anything more than a moment I can hold onto."

His hand stretched out on its own, brushing the hair from her neck. "You are…"

"What?" She rested her hands on his chest. "What am I, Nate?"

Everything stilled inside Nate's mind and body as he looked at her. She was beautiful. She was feisty and upbeat. And so wonderfully alive and real.

He could tell how she felt just by looking at her. Right then he could see that while she was only asking for the physical release from their attraction, she wanted so much more. She deserved more.

Nate looked into those soulful eyes and tried to loosen his hold on her waist. "You're not a one time deal."

She sucked in a breath. "How do you know? Maybe I am."

"Sweetheart," he pulled her in again to rest against him. "You're made to be held all night, every night. The man who gets to fall asleep and wake up with you will be very, very lucky."

He held her tight, listening to her mumble against him. "Don't you want it to be you?"

He knew without a doubt he did, but he was still torn.

She had to know everything. Maybe then he'd know if he could risk losing his heart again.

"Lilly, there's something I have to tell you."

*H*ow many times had her hopes been crushed by those words?

There's something I have to tell you.

They'd been followed by things like—I got a job offer, I'm moving, I met someone else. In the end, she'd never been that devastated, but somehow she worried it would be different this time. Sure, she'd tried to convince herself it didn't matter. It was just physical. But she knew better.

"Let's go inside where it's cooler then." Lilly removed herself from Nate's lap, embarrassed at her brazen attempt to seduce him. Her brief concern over what her mother would think was cut off with the realization she hadn't even succeeded at it. That thought made her laugh out loud.

"What's funny?" Nate asked.

"Nothing." Lilly shook her head and wondered if this was a story she'd ever get to share with her mama. "Have a seat. I'll get us some water."

"Wait." Nate grabbed her hand and pulled her to the couch. "If I don't tell you now I'll chicken out."

"You don't have to tell me." Lilly studied his face. There were circles under his eyes as if he hadn't slept, and that sadness she remembered from their first meetings had returned. That couldn't be good.

"I do. You deserve to know how messed up I am before you make any decisions. I don't want this attraction between us to factor into any of them." Nate traced his fingers down her cheek. "Remember, this is my running away place. It's time you knew what I was running away from."

Lilly tried to concentrate on what he said, but his touch kept distracting her. "What are you running away from Nate?"

Nate dropped his hand from her face, then pulled her to him, tucking her into his side. "My wife. Our baby."

Lilly gasped. She pushed away from him, landing on the floor. *"Estás casado! La dejaste a ella y a tu hijo?"*

"Slow down, I don't understand what you're saying." Nate reached for her.

"You're married?" She shoved his hands away and scrambled to her feet. "Don't touch me."

"Yes, no. This is coming out all wrong." Nate grabbed her, forcing her to stop retreating. "Would you listen to me?"

"¿Como pudiste? You have a child." Lilly tugged on her hands, but Nate held them firmly in his own. "You kissed me like you were free to do so."

"Lilly," his voice cracked. "They died two years ago. Meredith was my high school sweetheart, business partner, my everything."

Lilly flinched, but he didn't release his iron grip. The shock of that whispered phrase stole the rest of her breath. He wasn't married anymore, and he hadn't abandoned his child. Nate wasn't a cheater, but that woman had been his everything.

The anger at being used sagged out of her. A new hurt took its place. Why hadn't he said something before? Swallowing her own misery she asked, "What happened?"

"It was an accident, but she died, taking my world and our son with her."

The torment in his words was another blow to her heart. Lilly knew without a doubt he had loved his wife. The hitch in his voice was a testament to how much he still loved her.

Tears pricked her eyes. The knots worked their way up through her chest, straight to her head, where she struggled to keep it together.

He'd already found the love of his life. He couldn't be hers. If she was anything at all to him, she would always be his second. Second love, second chance, second choice, second best.

That thought gave her the strength to pull away. She couldn't put her heart on the line when she knew it could be crushed under that weight. She'd been second best all her life. In this one thing she needed to be first.

"Nate, I'm so sorry." Lilly backed further away, putting more space between them. This time he let her go. That hurt so bad.

"You're crying." He stepped forward, and she retreated to the door.

She wiped the tears from her cheeks. "I can tell how much you love her. How much you miss her."

"Now you understand why this is hard for me?" He tucked a strand of hair behind her ear.

Lilly nodded, but in truth, she had no idea. She'd never lost like he had. No, that wasn't true. She felt like she was losing now. More tears spilled down her face.

"Lilly?"

"*Necesito pensar.*"

"You need? What? Tell me." He pleaded with his eyes, but Lilly couldn't see past her own pain.

"*Necesito que me dejes en paz para que no rompas mi corazón más,*" Lilly almost choked on her own words. She opened the door and shoved him out.

"Lilly," he whispered before she closed the door on him.

She leaned against it for support. Then she gave in to the sobs. Her heart had broken before she'd even been sure it was in danger.

When she calmed down enough to speak, she tried to call her mama. When she didn't answer, Lilly cried in the message. "*Mama, te necesito.*"

Then she called her papi.

"What's wrong, *bebita?*" his strong voice soothed her.

"*Nada,* Papi. I miss you is all." Lilly curled up on the bed, hugging the pillow close. "Mama didn't answer her phone."

"I know, but she's softening. Today she asked if I'd heard from you. That's a good sign."

Lilly nodded even though he couldn't see and cried some more. "*Si*, it is."

"You could come home."

"I might." She choked on the next sob. "Very soon, Papi."

"*Buenas noches, te amo.*"

"I love you too, Papi." She hung up and waited to feel better.

When sleep didn't come, she lay in bed texting Selena and Gael until late in the night. Her brother offered to come and knock some sense into Nate even though he wasn't sure what the problem was.

He hurt her. Selena texted Gael.

Bcuz he wz married b4? he asked.

He didn't tell her.

But he wants Lil? And Lil wants him?

Lilly watched as Selena sent several frustrated emojis and tried to explain it to her brother, realizing that neither of them got it. If they didn't get it, maybe Nate didn't either.

Wanting wasn't enough.

Nate hadn't said he loved her. He'd said his wife had been his everything.

Eventually, she cried herself to sleep, not finding the comfort she needed.

THURSDAY

*L*illy woke Thursday morning with a headache and found medicine for it in the bathroom.

She would be okay. She'd have to be.

After swallowing the pills, she took herself upstairs, not even bothering to get dressed or eat breakfast. The first room was now organized in thirds—trash, donate, ask mom. It was time to tackle the second room.

There was a lot more of her grandmother's things in the second room. Especially the vintage dresses that went straight to her closet. Lilly had been sorting and only half paying attention to stuff when she found an old newspaper clipping.

LOCAL TEEN DEVELOPS NEW IRIS.

Under the headline was a photo of her mama and grandmother. They were both smiling, arms wrapped around each other, holding a potted iris between them. Lilly read the article twice before any of it sank in.

Abby had only been sixteen when she and grandma Lilly perfected the iris they'd created together. They'd named it

153

the Blue Josiah in honor of her grandpa who'd died only months before.

The article left Lilly with so many questions. How had they gone from happy to hate so quickly? She squinted at the faded black and white photo. It was strange to think that a few months later they'd go separate ways and never see each other again.

Her mama told her she hated gardening. Another lie!

Lilly pulled out her phone, snapped a picture of the article, and sent it to her mother.

Then she texted. **Plz call. Don't want 2 end up like u and grandma**.

Lilly sat and stared at the phone. Five minutes. Ten. It didn't ring, and there wasn't an answering text. The combined hurt and anger welled up.

Her mama hadn't answered a text or taken her calls for two weeks. Not even when she'd cried on the phone and told her she needed her. Maybe she should stop waiting for the day she was enough, because maybe her mother couldn't love her no matter what she did.

Lilly shoved a stack of boxes, knocking them over. A satisfying crash from inside one of them fueled her further. She pushed, threw, and slung things all over the room. Sobbing the whole time.

≈

*N*ate took a personal day at work. He'd messed things up so bad. By the end, he hadn't even known what Lilly was saying. She'd slipped into Spanish and he couldn't remember enough from high school to understand. It had been easier to leave, figuring she was better off without him.

She deserved someone who could devote himself to her

without making her cry. If only he could get those tears out of his memory.

He had Gypsy saddled and ready to go as soon as the sun was up. His plan was to wander the forty acres around Bear Mountain Stables, get lost, and forget everything.

Unfortunately, all he could think about was Lilly since he was riding her horse. He should have taken Blackberry, but Gyp needed exercise too.

Nate tried to think about Colorado instead. His parents wanted him to come back, but it didn't feel like home anymore. This felt like where he belonged. What if he got his vet's license for Arkansas? He could open his own practice. Settle in, really get to know the people here.

His pocket buzzed. He ignored it, glad when it stopped, but it started right up again. Nate pulled Gyp to a stop under some trees and tugged his phone out of his pocket. He had two missed calls. The last one from Flo.

"Aw, hell." He was still staring at it when she called again. "Hello."

"Nate, why aren't you answering your phone? Roberta tried to call you." Flo sounded breathless.

"I'm at work."

"Liar. Get off that horse and get over to Mrs. Lilly's. Somethin's going on," the fear in her voice sent a jolt straight to his heart.

He turned Gyp back toward the stables, maneuvering the woodland trail as fast as he could.

"What's going on?"

"I don't know. Roberta was taking some homemade bread, and she heard things smashing upstairs."

"Were there other cars there?"

"Just Lilly's, but town is full of strangers right now. You know how they wander where they're not supposed to."

"Did Roberta knock on the door?"

"She was scared to."

"I don't suppose she called the police." His fear eased a little.

"No, she thought of you first."

Nate grumbled, "We have a police department for a reason, but I'll check on her. My guess is she just knocked something over."

"Roberta said she heard lots of things breaking," Flo's voice leveled out. "And she heard crying."

It sounded more and more like a fit to him.

"Mrs. DeWitt. What are you two up to?" Nate continued down the trail, but he let Gyp slow to her own pace.

"You'd better take this seriously. If that girl's been murdered in her grandma's house, it'll be your fault."

"How will it be my fault?" He almost turned around, knowing he'd lose cell service somewhere out there.

"We heard you two had a fight. Now get over there and apologize." Florence hung up the phone.

Nate chuckled. The busybodies in town were up to trouble again. Still, better safe than sorry, and he wanted to see her.

It took another ten minutes to reach the stables. He rushed through brushing Gyp and giving her feed and water, but a good half hour passed before he pulled into Mrs. Lilly's drive.

Lilly's car was gone.

Momentary relief hit him. He hadn't been sure what to say, especially after the emotional dismissal the night before.

Roberta's claim of breaking glass had him curious though, so he got out and knocked. When no one answered, he pulled out his key and stepped inside, flicking on the lights.

Downstairs didn't look any worse for wear. He noticed the door leading up was open. When he reached it he let out a low whistle. Papers littered the steps along with other random items. He picked his way to the top.

"Yeah, definitely throwing a fit." The carnage in the room smacked of the passion he'd seen burning in her eyes a couple of times. "What brought this on?"

Nate found her phone against the wall, a good size crack running down the screen. He heard the front door open.

"Nate! *Sal de me casa!*"

Definitely on fire, and not murdered in her house. He didn't move since he heard the angry clatter of her steps coming up. She appeared holding a box of trash bags and a broom.

"You gonna club me with that?" he asked.

"Maybe. What right do you have to let yourself in here?" she glared, then dropped the box and held out her hand. "Give me the key."

"I don't think I will." He shoved his hands in his pockets and studied her. She had circles under her eyes. They were puffy, as if she hadn't stopped crying after he left.

Is that my fault?

Lilly practically buzzed with anger. Her face was twisted up, her breathing ragged. Just looking at her had his heart pounding and every part of him aching to hold her close. He needed to get out quick or he'd forget he was supposed to let her go.

"Nate Pierce, give me the key or I'm calling the police." She waved the extended hand in his direction.

"No, ma'am." He stepped past her and retreated downstairs, pausing only a moment at the door. "I'll let Roberta and Flo know you weren't murdered."

Then he vacated her property, closing the door behind him. She'd been storming in his direction and closing it only slowed her down. He could hear her fumbling with the latch

157

as he walked toward his truck and knew the moment she opened it.

Nate didn't turn, just kept walking. It came as a surprise when she swatted him with the broom.

"What the hell?" he roared, and turned to see her holding the offending object like a baseball bat. "I don't know what bee got up your nose, but you need to calm down."

"What bee…" her nostrils flared and he thought she might take another swing at him. "Give me the key."

"I said no." He stood his ground, ready to grab for the broom if she came at him again.

She didn't though. Instead, she sucked in a breath and ran for the house. He caught her on the porch steps.

"Lilly, what's going on?"

"Go away. If you don't respect me enough to give me a stupid key, I don't want to see you."

"Lilly—"

"I said go away!"

Mere never threw a fit like this.

Nate sighed and backed off. "If that's what you want."

"None of us get what we want, Nate."

That stopped him in his tracks. "What are you talking about?"

"Not my mom, not her parents, not me, and not you. So it doesn't really matter does it?"

Now she was scaring him. "What doesn't matter, Lilly?"

"What we want. It doesn't matter. Go home, Nate. I'm done competing with everyone living and dead. From now on I can only be me, and that has to be enough." Lilly stepped through the door and slammed it.

She didn't lock it. It was like she knew he wouldn't force his way in again.

He may have convinced Lilly he didn't care, but he knew

more than ever that his need to comfort her bordered on obsessive. And that would only hurt her more in the end.

Nate turned for his truck. Man, it sucked doing the right thing.

~

*L*illy felt stupid for crying in front of Nate. She couldn't hold in the anger, hurt, and helplessness. It was like she'd lost all control over her life. Her mom wouldn't talk to her after lying for years, she'd finally fallen in love with a man that wouldn't fight for her, and all her siblings knew what they wanted out of life but she didn't.

She was floundering. Helping at Eric's house had been the most fulfilling thing she'd done in a long time, but the fact she'd been with Nate tainted it. How could she know if she'd enjoyed the job or the company?

And she'd stupidly fallen for him. A man with baggage. One that seemed to enjoy pushing her buttons and then telling her no.

The worst part was she hadn't even realized she was doing it. She'd convinced herself it was only physical attraction, mostly, right up until he'd mentioned his wife. Lust didn't leave your heart bruised and bleeding when someone walked away. She'd never felt such anguish or loneliness before.

When Nate refused to give her the key it had simply been the last straw.

Lilly wiped at her tears. It was time to take charge of her own life. Make her own decisions. Her mother wasn't talking to her anyway, so what did it matter if she approved or not? She would just have to find something else that would make her happy. In the meantime, she'd clean up her mess.

*N*ate worried about Lilly all day Friday while he worked. The guys teased him about the rumors he'd dated and broken up with Lilly all in a week. He perfected his glare and they backed off until they split for their different jobs.

The worst part was they got to enjoy harassing him and all he could do was miss her. He missed her so much he went to Eric's house just to be somewhere they'd been happy together. It was pathetic.

"Hey, Nate." Eric waved from his yard. "Do you need something?"

"I wanted to check if the water feature was working correctly. Sometimes they malfunction."

"It's been fine. Come on back though."

Nate climbed out of the truck and followed. The air was dense with memories. Nate wondered if Eric was thinking about the disaster at the party, but he was determined not to bring it up. It wasn't any of his business, and Kerri and Eric had seemed fine at the lake.

"So, you and Lilly coming to Kerri's tonight to make

chocolates?" Eric asked.

Nate stopped in his tracks. He'd forgotten all about that. "Probably not, considering Lilly chased me off her property with a broom."

"What?" Eric laughed. "When was this?"

"Yesterday, around noon."

Eric sobered. "Huh. I sort of thought you two might, uh, you know."

"Nope."

"Sorry, man. I'll leave you to it." Eric waved at the pond and backed away, leaving Nate alone.

Lilly really had done a great job with the landscaping. He remembered how she'd glowed as she organized everyone. She knew exactly where she wanted the plants, how the beds should be placed, even the height of the water feature levels. And she'd worked as hard as the men, never expecting anyone to do something she wasn't willing to do herself.

He'd almost kissed her over there. She'd been swaying her hips and talking about starting fires. Her kiss fulfilled that promise, but her smile warmed his heart.

She'd been excited to help Kerri with the chocolate class. It wasn't his thing, but maybe if he could get her to go, he'd get another chance with her.

After checking the pump on the waterfall, Nate jogged around to the front. Eric was sitting in his car, the door still open.

"What time should we be at Kerri's? And can I get an address?"

Eric frowned and held up his phone. "Kerri just texted that she isn't feeling good. She's having a flare-up so I don't think the class is a good idea."

"Oh, okay." There went his second chance.

Eric kept talking, "When Kerri's RA flares up we sit and watch a movie. Which means she sleeps and I end up watching ESPN. She probably wouldn't care if you hung out with us to keep me from being bored."

"Are you sure?"

"Hold on." Eric typed on his phone. After a minute he looked up and smiled. "She's cool with it."

Nate sighed. It wouldn't solve his problem with Lilly, but it would give him time to think. He scratched the back of his neck. "Okay, thanks."

Eric reached into the console, grabbed a pen and scribbled something. "Here's Kerri's address. Show up around seven."

Nate got through the rest of his day without cutting his foot off in a mower or anything else stupid. He cleaned his apartment, shopped for groceries, and stared at the TV after his shower. It wasn't even on, but he didn't know what else to do. Lilly stayed in his thoughts the whole time.

What he felt for her was more than attraction. It ran deeper than that. She made him want to rejoin the living again. Do more than just survive from day to day. He could have a life with her like he had with Meredith. It would be different, maybe even better.

That thought scared him and brought the guilt back. He'd promised Meredith there'd never be another woman for him. But she was gone. Was it wrong to want a second chance at happiness? What if Lilly didn't give him another chance?

"Hang out with Eric and forget it for one night," he mumbled and headed into town.

Kerri lived about half a mile from Eric's, but there was nowhere to park. After driving past the little house twice, Nate parked at Eric's and walked. By the time he reached the yard, he was covered in sweat.

Lilly stood on the porch, hand poised to knock. He cleared his throat, and she turned to stare at him.

"What are you doing here?" she hissed as her brow arched upward.

She wore a black and white polka dot dress with red roses scattered over it. Her makeup was light, but bright red lipstick drew his eyes straight to her lips. She had curled her hair.

"Wow." He ran up the steps.

She stumbled backward. "Why are you here?"

She sounded breathless. He wanted to reach for her, but the panic in her eyes kept him at arm's length.

A new thought slammed into Nate's head. "You're really dressed up. Are you meeting someone else?"

The surprised look on her face was classic. "Someone else? Nate, that's just." She stared at him. "You don't get it do you?"

"Explain it to me." A little irritation slipped into his voice.

"There isn't anyone else, but I can't let you keep hurting me." She twisted her hands in front of her. "That's why I have to go back to Dallas."

Nate froze. If she left he wouldn't have time to fix this. "You don't have to leave. I'll stay away. You can finish going through the house, do whatever you want around town. I'll stay away."

"Nate—"

The door swung open.

Kerri stood there, pale with dark circles under her eyes, Eric hovering close behind. "Oh, no. Lilly, I'm so sorry. I forgot to tell you."

"Tell me what?" Lilly focused on Kerri, carefully avoiding Nate.

"I canceled the chocolate class."

"I should have given you my phone number." Lilly touched Kerri's arm. "Why did you cancel?"

Kerri blushed and looked at the ground. Eric wrapped his arms around her. She grimaced and Eric backed away.

"Does that hurt?" Eric asked her.

Kerri gazed up at him and spoke softly, "Sorry."

"No, I'm sorry." Eric kissed the tip of her nose and then backed away. Kerri stretched her fingers to brush his hand for a moment before letting them rest by her side again.

Nate felt a pang of longing. Not for Kerri, but for the closeness the two obviously shared.

Eric smiled at her. "Kerri overdid it yesterday and is paying for it today."

"What do you mean?" Lilly looked back and forth between the couple.

"It's my arthritis. Sometimes I get really sore and achy, then I just want to curl up and sleep." Kerri leaned into her boyfriend a little more. "I went shopping and visited the museum and trails in Bentonville yesterday."

"Oh, I'm sorry, but I understand." Lilly fidgeted beside him. "Well, I'll head home then. I hope you feel better."

"Nonsense. We should do the class. You're both here, and I won't be doing the work. If you leave, I'll just sit here thinking about the pain. This way I'm distracted." Kerri beckoned them inside.

"Kerri, this isn't a good idea," Lilly pleaded.

"We can always reschedule." Nate placed his hand on Lilly's lower back. She stiffened under his touch but didn't pull away. "You guys enjoy your night."

Eric winked at Nate. "You too. Maybe we can all go out some other time?"

"But—" Kerri protested.

"If you want, you can teach me to make chocolates again," Eric spoke close to Kerri's ear, and she turned bright red.

"Night, Lilly." Kerri closed the door without another word.

As soon as they were alone, Lilly moved away from his touch and hurried down the steps.

"Lilly, wait."

"Nate, please just let me go."

"Sure, after you get to your car." He kept pace easily and searched for something to say. "So, what's with getting all dressed up?"

She let out a strangled laugh. "Sometimes a girl needs to get dolled up to feel better. You have a problem with that?"

~

"*Y*ou must feel great looking like that." His voice had gone low and sexy.

Lilly's heart pounded. If she weren't wearing the cute red opera stilettos, she would run. As it was, she had to go slower on the uneven sidewalk, forcing her to stay close enough for that voice to have power over her.

"So, why were you throwing a fit yesterday?"

"Has my tantrum been bothering you?" Lilly was proud her voice almost sounded normal.

"Maybe." His murmur continued to wreak havoc with her insides.

Lilly found it harder and harder to breathe. She needed to break the spell he was putting her under and let him know not everything was about him.

"It shouldn't." She sucked in a deep breath and walked faster. "I reached my limit with Abby. I'm done begging for her to talk to me. When she's ready, I'll answer, but it's in her court now."

"Oh." He took hold of her arm and pulled her to a stop. "That's all?"

Lilly bristled. "Should there be anything else?"

"Come on, we need to talk about this." He pointed between them.

"No, we don't." She jerked herself free and continued down the hill toward town.

"When I told you about Meredith, I was trying to be honest with you. It's the only way I know how to move forward. Be honest with me." He grabbed her again, staring down at her, not giving an inch. "Tell me what's wrong between us."

Lilly struggled to breathe. The truth threatened to spill. Maybe then she could accept it and move on, but oh how it would hurt. Speaking it aloud would make it a reality.

"Please, Lilly."

She clapped her hand over her mouth, desperate to hold the pain inside. Her vision blurred, but she blinked it away.

Nate caressed the side of her face. "What am I doing wrong?"

"You found it, they've found it." She waved back toward Kerri's.

Nate pulled her in close and wrapped his arms around her. She could feel him breathing, hear his heart beating fast under her ear. He rested his head on hers and sighed.

"Be patient."

"Be patient?" Lilly shoved herself away. "I'm twenty-eight for crying out loud. How long am I supposed to wait?"

The hill grew steeper, but she tottered down it.

Didn't Nate realize he made her feel things she'd never felt before? But he didn't say he cared about her in any way comparable to his wife. He'd given no indication he might one day love her.

"Lilly, wait."

"Be patient. Wait. That's all you ever say, but you don't tell me what I'm waiting for. Go home, Nate. Leave me alone."

"Fine. I love you."

Lilly stopped and placed her hands on her hips. *"Gracias por nada."*

"Thanks for nothing? I just said I love you." Nate's brow wrinkled.

"Very convincingly too." She bent and slipped off her heels. Once they were in her hand she used them to shove him back a step. "Do. Not. Follow me, Nate."

She spun and jogged the last block to her car. Once inside, she cranked up the air and rolled down the windows to push out the heat. She held in the tears until she made it home.

Fine. I love you.

Who could ask for a better declaration of love than that?

Lilly crawled into bed and cried herself to sleep knowing she couldn't stay in Eureka Springs any longer. Even if Nate kept his promise and stayed away, there would be memories of him all over town. And there would always be the possibility of running into him.

SATURDAY

Since she decided to go back to Dallas, Lilly spent the morning packing the car with things to take home. Then she asked Flo to send her husband to pick up all the things for donation. He had to make several trips, but the house emptied quickly with his help. They also carried two truckloads or junk to a dump. It was mid-afternoon by the time they finished.

Lilly showered before seeking out some of her new friends to say goodbye to.

She took her time. There were no more tears. Time for that had passed. She couldn't change the way she felt, and she couldn't change the way Nate felt. All she could do was go about her life the best she could.

Eventually, she'd have to return and finish things here, but right now she needed her familiar, boring life. She'd go to work, she'd hang out with her friends. Maybe even go on a date with the guy who kept coming to the flower shop. Even though he didn't make her feel anything.

She'd go see her mama. Take her the things she'd found at

Mrs. Lilly's. And if Abby still didn't talk to her, that would be okay.

None of it mattered. She would have to do her best and find her own happiness in the end. No one else could give it to her. She'd turn off all her emotions until the pain subsided.

Lilly made sure all the windows were closed and locked, the curtains pulled shut. She loved the little house. The flower beds looked nicer than when she'd arrived thanks to the mornings she'd spent tending it. The field had grown quickly over the last two weeks. When would Nate come to mow again? She wished she could watch him with his shirt off from the upstairs window one more time.

Stop it. But she didn't want to stop thinking about him. That's why she had to leave.

She paused halfway down the drive to look at the field again. It was the perfect place for greenhouses. If she could stand to be in the same town as Nate she could start her own business, get into landscaping for real. Or at least into growing plants and supplying local flower shops.

"Maybe when I get over him." She tucked the idea to the back of her mind again. The land was hers, and it would keep.

Lilly found Kerri at her mom's bead shop in town.

"Hey, how are you today?" Kerri asked when she walked in.

"I was going to ask you the same thing." Lilly gave the other woman a hug.

"Tired, but not as sore. Eric made me do yoga this morning. I have a love-hate relationship with yoga." She wrinkled her nose. "Hate doing it, but love that I feel better after."

"I totally understand." Lilly studied the little shop for a minute before focusing back on Kerri. "I actually came to say goodbye. I'm heading home tonight."

"No!" Kerri jumped up from her stool and gave Lilly a real hug. "I guess things didn't work out with Nate?"

"No. It's okay." Lilly fumbled with some blue beads in a container by the register. "It'll be okay."

"Well, come back and visit us sometime."

"I will. Can you tell the others bye for me? All of you were so nice to welcome me to town. I'll never forget our day on the lake."

"I bet Nate won't either. In fact, I think it'll haunt him." She climbed back on the seat. "Serves him right. I can't believe he's letting you leave."

Lilly shrugged.

"Are you at least leaving him your number?"

"He doesn't even know I'm leaving. It's better this way."

"Lilly, you have to give him a chance. What if he just needs a wake-up call?"

Lilly cocked her head to the side and pointed at Kerri. "You're one to talk. You've got a great guy who adores you, would do anything for you, and you told him no."

Kerri jumped off the seat and grabbed a broom. "That's different."

"I don't see how."

"I'm sick." Kerri started sweeping with a vengeance.

"He doesn't care."

"I care."

Lilly took the broom from her. "Kerri, it's none of my business, but don't throw happiness away because you're scared. Life is hard enough as it is. Don't make it harder. Eric just wants a chance to show you how much you mean to him. He wants to make your life easier."

"But he shouldn't have to."

"Ah, so that's it."

"Yes. I should be able to take care of myself."

"Then do it, but let him be there too. I'm leaving and I

don't even know if my mother will be a part of my life. Do you know how much I'd give to have someone standing beside me for this? I know I can do it on my own, but to have someone hold my hand would be..." Lilly swiped at a tear. "I thought I was done crying. Kerri, let Eric hold your hand. Don't be stupid."

Kerri hugged her again. "Thanks, Lilly. I hope you find someone to hold your hand."

"Me too."

"Oh, what are you going to do about Gypsy? Wasn't Nate taking care of her?"

Lilly's shoulders sagged. "Yeah. I'll stop by Bear Mountain on my way out. Maybe I can work something out with them. Nate shouldn't have to keep doing it for free."

"Are you going now?"

Lilly glanced at her phone. It was already after six. "Yeah, it's getting late and it's a long drive home."

"Okay. Drive safe, and don't be a stranger."

"Here," Lilly texted her address to Kerri, "I expect a wedding invitation."

Kerri blushed. "I'll work on that."

$\sim$

*N*ate watched the sky. A storm was rolling in. It hadn't rained in over three weeks and they needed the rain. The lakes and reservoirs were fine, but that wouldn't last if the summer stayed dry. This looked like a beast of a storm though moving in fast. He turned the radio station in his truck to catch the forecast, but his phone rang, cutting in on the bluetooth.

"This is Pierce."

"Hi Nate, it's Kerri."

"What's up?"

"Just thought you'd like to know that Lilly was just in to say goodbye. Sounds like she's heading home to Dallas tonight."

Nate's world stood still. She was leaving. He shouldn't be surprised. She said she needed to. It was his fault. All because he wanted her but was too scared to keep her.

"Nate?"

He cleared his throat. "Thanks for letting me know."

"Nate, you can ask her to stay. Do you want her to stay?"

"It doesn't matter what I want."

"I'll tell you what she told me. Don't be stupid. She's in love with you. If you want her to stay, all you have to do is ask."

"But she's already headed out."

"No, she's stopping to make arrangements for Gypsy. You can catch her at Bear Mountain."

He'd thrown the truck in reverse and headed down Hwy. 62 before she'd finished. "Thanks, Kerri."

It took forever to navigate the tourist traffic out of town. He kept praying they were just as busy at the stables, that it would take a while for someone to help Lilly square things away. Never mind she didn't want him taking care of Gyp anymore. Would it be so hard to talk to him?

He was relieved to see Lilly's car in the parking lot when he arrived. It was loaded down with boxes, but at least he hadn't missed her. He ran into the stable, thinking she might be at Gypsy's stall, but it was empty. Back outside, he saw a group coming in from the trail. They wouldn't know where she'd gone. Nate headed to the office, hoping to find someone who'd have more information.

He finally found Michael in a back paddock training one of the new horses. Nate hopped up on the fence.

"Hey, have you seen Lilly today? She was coming to see Gyp."

"I didn't see her, but I think Jim did. He left about ten minutes ago with a group." Michael came closer, leading the young horse with a rope. "He should have a walkie with him. Channel 4."

"Thanks." Nate ran back to the stable. In the front office, he grabbed one of the walkie-talkies. It was already set to the correct channel. "Jim, this is Nate at Bear Mountain, come in."

He waited only a minute before the reply. "Yeah, Nate, this is Jim."

"Did you see Lilly this afternoon?"

"Yeah, I helped her saddle Gypsy. She wanted to take one more ride before going back to Texas."

"You did what?" Nate glanced out the door, hoping to see Lilly walking in. "Is she with you now?"

"No, said she wanted to be alone."

"Jim, she's only been on a horse twice."

"Well, I didn't know that. She acted like she knew what she was doing." The line crackled a minute, then Jim came back on. "Look there's a storm coming in. I'm bringing my group back. She headed down toward Lake Leatherwood. You should go after her."

"Darn right I'm going after her." Nate had already grabbed his saddle and shoved the walkie and a water bottle in a pack. "Hey Blackberry, time to go find the old lady and bring her home."

He talked to the horse the whole time he saddled him. It calmed Nate enough to pull out his phone and try calling Lilly. She didn't answer, but he couldn't be sure if that was because she didn't have reception or because she didn't want to talk to him. He called Kerri and asked her to call Lilly. She didn't have any luck reaching her either.

Nate led Blackberry out of the barn. "Okay, we have to assume she's lost reception. That's going to make it harder to find her and we're going to get caught in this storm. Get some help out here, and can you find her parents' number? It's time her mom started talking to her daughter again."

"I'll work on it. And Nate, good luck."

"Thanks, Kerri."

Nate hit the trail Jim had indicated at a trot. The storm clouds had moved in, making the shaded pathway dark and treacherous. He wanted to move faster, but low tree branches made that unwise.

His main concern was Lilly. If it had been light, Gyp could have brought her home, but the horse was blind in the dark. The worst part was Nate hadn't told Lilly about Gypsy's night blindness yet. That could put both of them in more danger.

Lilly didn't know anything about the land or horses. And now the storm was going to add poor visibility making Gyp nervous. The walkie crackled in the pack.

"Nate, this is Michael at Bear Mountain, come in."

Nate stretched to reach the pouch and pull the walkie out. "This is Nate."

"We've got search and rescue out on horses and four-wheelers covering the other trails."

"Thanks."

"Also, the storm hit with lightning first and started a forest fire to the north. The good news is rain followed so it isn't spreading. Just be careful out there."

"Okay, thanks again. Is everyone on this channel?"

"Yes."

"Good, keep me posted. Out."

Nate replaced the walkie and took a swig of water. The humidity had risen to swelter level. He wondered if Lilly had water with her.

He cupped his hands and yelled. "Lilly!"

Blackberry's ears twitched, but there was no other

response. Nate moved on down the trail. It seemed like Mrs. Lilly's ghost had abandoned him ever since he'd started liking her granddaughter.

"Mrs. Lilly, shame on you. She needs our help. Why don't you at least point me in the right direction."

He strained to listen, to feel a breeze, smell her perfume, anything.

There was nothing.

The sky grew darker and split open. Rain poured down in bucketfuls. It didn't cool things off, just made everything sticky and sodden. He wished for one of his old cowboy hats to keep the rain out of his eyes.

The ground rumbled at the same time a loud crack reverberated through his bones.

"That was close." Nate slid off Blackberry and led him with the reins. How far could Lilly have gone?

He hadn't prayed in two years. Not since he'd lost Mere and his baby boy. He did now. He prayed Lilly was safe. That he would find her soon. That she would let him hold her and bring her home.

Another bolt of lightning illuminated the sky. The thunder rolled through his feet the way he imagined an earthquake would.

When Kerri told him Lilly was leaving, he thought he wanted to say goodbye. Now he knew he wanted to ask her to stay. He needed her in his life. Nate still didn't know how to reconcile that with his love for Meredith, but he knew his home was with Lilly.

Nathaniel, loving her doesn't mean you didn't love me.

Nate stumbled. The rain slowed, and it sounded muffled in his ears. It was as if the whole world had stopped moving.

Meredith? He strained to hear her again.

Find Lilly and be happy.

It *was* his wife's voice. A warmth filled his heart. Meredith had given her blessing. The guilt he'd been holding onto washed away with the water running down his face.

"Thank you, Mere," he said.

He also smelled Mrs. Lilly's perfume. It drifted to him from the left of the trail and down the hill.

As he searched the side of the path, he noticed a side trail leading down. Some of the dirt was gouged out as if something big had slid down it. When he found it, the rushing sound of rain returned with another crack of thunder and lightning.

"Come on boy." He carefully led his horse down the steep embankment. At the bottom, he yelled again. "Lilly!"

～

illy hadn't planned on taking a ride before leaving town, but when she saw the horse huffing in her stall she couldn't help it. One of the men helped her saddle Gypsy. A quick stroll down one of the shorter trails couldn't hurt anything.

"You know I don't want to leave, don't you girl?" Lilly sighed and flexed her fingers. She'd been on the trail for twenty minutes, but her nerves hadn't calmed down. In fact, her hands shook more now than before. "But I can't stay."

She enjoyed the breeze and let the horse walk at her own pace not having to work to keep her on the trail. It was nice to trust Gyp and let her mind mull over her problem with Nate.

Lilly loved him. There was no denying it. He was attracted to her and liked her on some level. Would that be enough? Could she settle for friendship and chemistry just to be with him?

His words about his wife echoed in her mind. *She was my everything.*

The ache inside told her friendship would never be enough. She wanted to be someone's everything. To be their whole world the way she thought Nate might have become hers.

"It's not fair, Gyp," Lilly pouted.

A low rumble of thunder sounded in the distance. Lilly pulled Gypsy to a stop. She'd been so caught up in her thoughts she hadn't noticed the dark clouds rolling in. They were moving fast with the wind that had felt so good earlier.

Lilly struggled to get Gypsy turned around and heading back the way she'd come. Not because Gypsy was uncooperative, but because Lilly wasn't as familiar with how to move the reins to communicate what she wanted. Once they were facing in the right direction, Lilly sighed with relief.

Five minutes later, the storm moved overhead. The wind kicked up, and the sky darkened like night beneath the canopy of trees. Gypsy barely moved.

"Come on, girl. We've got to keep going." Lilly lightly flicked the reins to no avail. Gypsy had lowered her head to the ground. No matter how hard Lilly pulled, she couldn't get the horse to lift her head. "Gypsy?"

Another crack of thunder exploded above them. Gypsy startled and made a sound like a scream. Lilly held on tight when the horse jerked. Luckily, Gypsy didn't break into a run.

Then the rain started. It didn't start slowly. It was more like someone flicked a switch and sheets of water poured from the sky. Lilly's hair and clothes were drenched in a minute. Her sneakers squelched in the stirrups, and the water in her eyes made it almost impossible to see anything.

"Gypsy, you have to get us back." Lilly nudged the horse with her heels and flicked the reins again.

The horse took a shuffling step to the side and lost her footing.

Everything paused. Lilly felt as if she were floating, then she hit the ground. The air rushed from her lungs. She scrambled to grab onto something as she slid down a hillside, grateful Gypsy hadn't stepped on her. Branches and rocks scraped and pummeled her body until she came to rest in the mud at the bottom.

"Gyp?" Lilly moaned and sat up. Nothing was broken, but she knew her body would hurt in the morning. She slowly crawled to her feet and looked for her horse.

Gypsy stood close by, covered in mud and scratches, nose still to the ground. Her ears swiveled all around as she snorted.

"What happened, girl?" Lilly approached carefully. The horse took tiny steps, her ears in constant motion as if she were trying to figure things out by sound. "Whoa, it's just me."

Lilly picked up the reins from the ground. There was no way she could get back in the saddle on her own. It wouldn't matter anyway. Gypsy was scared, and Lilly was no longer sure which way would take them back to the stable. She tugged on the horses head, trying to get Gyp's nose off the ground.

The rain continued to pour down. Even though it was still hot, Lilly shivered. She was stuck. Gypsy wouldn't move.

"Fine. Stay here. I'll be back." Frustrated, Lilly dropped the reins and walked back to the hill.

She didn't think she could crawl up it. Water ran down in muddy rivulets. Instead, she found the trail and followed it away from the hill.

A couple hundred feet down, she discovered a natural rock wall rising from the ground. At one point, it jutted out, making a natural umbrella. Now, if she could only get Gypsy over to it.

Lilly prayed, swore in two languages, pushed, and pulled,

but eventually, she got Gypsy to the overhang. By then, her arms trembled, and she had to lean against the wall because she didn't think her legs would hold her up any longer.

She tied Gyp to a tree and moved a couple feet away from her. It broke her heart, but every time it thundered, or lightning ripped through the sky, the horse would jump and bump into the side of the hill.

"Lilly?" the voice sounded like it was coming from far away.

"Here, I'm over here!" she yelled. There was no answer. She waited, her heart pounding, the rain sounding like static. "Hello? Can you hear me?"

"Lilly?" The voice was closer this time.

"I'm over here!" She ran toward the voice.

A shape formed in the gray woods. It was a man, leading a horse. He was soaking wet, but she recognized his walk before she ever saw the features of his face.

"Nate!"

"Lilly, are you okay?" He left his horse and ran to her.

Before she could answer, he had her face in his hands. He turned her head this way and that. Then he examined her shoulders, arms, ran his hands down her sides, letting them rest on her hips, while his eyes continued down her legs.

"You're staring at my legs again," Her voice caught and she swallowed.

"You'd better get used to that." Nate stepped closer, pressing her body against his.

"Why?" She stared up at him tired of running from what she wanted, knowing she should.

He lifted her off the ground bringing her eye level. She had to wrap her arms and legs around him for support.

"Lilly Ramirez, you can't leave."

"Oh, Nate." *Give me more*. Silently she begged to hear the right words from him.

"No, listen to me. I need you in my life. You make me happy. You make me better."

"Nate, I don't want you to feel guilty when you're with me," she swallowed, "and I don't want to feel like I'm second best."

"I won't, and you're not," Nate growled. "I'm doing this all wrong."

"Just tell me the truth. You didn't want to like me because you felt you were cheating on your wife."

"Yes. At first. Be patient while I try to explain."

"Ug, not this again." Lilly tried to push away.

"Wait."

"Nate, this is Jim, come in." There was a squawking sound from Nate's horse.

"Aw, hell. I forgot about the other search parties." Nate set Lilly down. "Give me a minute."

He dug a walkie-talkie from his saddlebag. "Jim, this is Nate. I've found her. Looks like she took the east spur trail off the Leatherwood Lake trail. Everyone can head back to the stable. Out."

"Good. Need assistance?"

Nate looked at her. When she shook her head he replied, "No, we're good."

"Okay, see you soon. Out."

Nate put the walkie-talkie away and turned back to her. "Now, where were we?"

"Hopefully, going home."

His brow went up, but she turned and retreated to where she'd left Gypsy.

"Lilly?"

"What?"

"Are you scared of me?"

"*Si escucho, me romperás el corazón.*"

"All I got from that was break and heart." He cupped her

face with his hand. "Lilly, I've never wanted to break your heart. That's what I was the most afraid of. Yes, I loved my wife, and yes, I felt like I was being disloyal to her. Let me tell you why."

He waited, almost like he was asking permission to continue. Lilly nodded. Her heart pounded and sent a silent plea heavenward, *let me be enough*.

"Meredith and I were always good together. Happy. But when I touch you, kiss you, it's fire and passion like I've never felt. I didn't know how to explain that. How to make that okay without making what I had with her less. Does that make sense?"

"You've never felt this before either?" Lilly's heart soared. Maybe she was more than enough. She gazed into his eyes, hoping against hope she might finally get her happily ever after.

"No. Meredith may have been my first girlfriend and wife, but what I feel with you is so different it can't be compared. She was a comfortable best friend. This all consuming fire is a first for me."

Lilly sucked in a breath. She was a first. "Really?"

"I meant what I said. The man who gets to be with you will be very lucky. I'm asking you to let it be me."

"So what exactly are you asking me leg guy?" She rested her hands on his strong chest.

"I'm asking you to marry me as soon as we can get our families to this crazy little town. I don't want to wait. I want to get married, open a new veterinarian clinic, and be stupid happy with you."

"Yes, to all of that! And, can we live at Mrs. Lilly's? I want to put in greenhouses and grow tons and tons of flowers."

Nate swung her around, dousing them both with more rain. "As long as you let me put in central air conditioning."

Lilly answered him with a kiss. When they came up for

air she said, "Only if you agree to mow the yard without your shirt."

"I thought you were watching that day."

"I was trying to be discreet with my gawking."

Nate laughed before moving in for another kiss.

SUNDAY

*S*unday morning dawned sunny and hot. Everything was bright and green, the dust had been washed away by the storm and life looked wonderful. Lilly was almost ready for church when someone knocked on the door.

"Nate you're half an hour early. It's unlocked. Not that that should stop you." She hollered down the hall and made another pass over her hair with the flat iron.

She heard the door open and close.

"Lilliana?" a woman's voice drifted down the hall.

She dropped the comb in the sink and the iron clattered on the counter. Lilly poked her head around the bathroom door. Sure enough, her mama and papi stood just inside her foyer.

Her parents were here! Joy coursed through here even though they weren't smiling. At least, her mama wasn't, but Papi wore his secret little smile. The one that told her he was happy even if Abby didn't think he should be.

"*Estas Aqui*! Why didn't you call?" She ran down the hall and hugged her father. "Papi, what are you doing here?"

He left his arm around her waist and looked her over. "A man called and said you were lost in a storm and we needed to get up here. It's good to see you're safe."

"Was this some trick of yours to get me here?" Her mama's brow creased, and she folded her arms across her chest.

"No, Mama! I don't even know who called you. If you don't want to be here you can leave." Lilly clung to her papi, the hurt rising to the surface again. "Why do you hate me, Mama? Am I so much like her that you could never love me as much as Maria or Selena?"

"Lilly," Papi scolded. "You know your mama loves you."

"Does she?" Lilly met her mama's gaze. "Do you?"

Her mother stared at her, blinking several times before answering. "I've always loved you. I just want you to find yourself. Figure out how you're going to make your mark on the world. That's why I push so hard."

"Really?" Lilly sagged in her papi's arms. "But why didn't you return my calls the last few weeks?"

Abby glanced at the floor. "I was embarrassed."

"Embarrassed? Is that why grandma died never having talked to any of her grandchildren?" Lilly broke away from her papi and stood in front of her mother. "Mama, you've got four other children to take my place, but you were all she had. She died alone, thinking you hated her. Was that because you were embarrassed?"

"Lilly," Jose sounded sad, but he no longer fussed. He took his wife in his arms. "You don't have to be so harsh."

"But she needs to hear it, Papi. She needs to know that could have been us. What if something had happened to me last night? What if I had died thinking Mama hated me?" Lilly touched her mama's arm. "Mama, I love you. I need you, but you have to be there."

"I'm sorry." Abby turned and hugged Lilly close. "I promise I'll do better. Keep reminding me."

Lilly felt how tight her mama held on. It squeezed all the pain and anger right out of her. The relief of it brought tears to her own eyes, and she hugged her back.

"I will, Mama."

They held each other several minutes before Papi pulled them apart.

He took each by the hand. "That's my girls. It's about time." Jose kissed his wife before looking his daughter over again. "Look at you. You look different. What is it, Mama?"

"She's in love." Abby smiled at her, and for once, Lilly felt it was genuine.

Lilly touched her cheeks, feeling how warm they'd become. "How can you tell?"

"A mama knows. I suspected when you left your message, but when that man called I knew." Her eyes sparkled. "He makes you happy?"

"You mentioned someone called. Was it Nate?"

"Yes. He said you needed us, that you had reminded him that family was everything," Papi said it proudly.

Lilly felt her heart swell even more. Nate had brought her mama to her. "Yes, Mama. Nate makes me happy. He got you here, didn't he?"

"This is true." Abby's smile hadn't faded. "When will we get to meet him?"

"He should be here soon." Lilly waved a hand around the entryway to the two living rooms. "Has it changed much, Mama?"

She watched her mom look around. "Not much."

"I have boxes of stuff for you. Things grandma kept that you might like."

"Maybe we can go through it together later." Abby leaned

into Jose. "Tell us more about your plans. When are you coming home?"

Just then Nate appeared at the door with a box of pastries. "Morning, I see you have company. Good thing I brought extras."

Lilly hurried to him, giddy just to see him. "Nate, these are my parents. Abby and Jose Ramirez, this is Nate Pierce, my fiancé."

"Fiancé?" Her mother's brow shot up. "When did that happen?"

"Last night." Lilly reached for Nate's hand.

"But he hasn't asked your father's permission."

"Seriously, Mama? Papi's here so we can do that now if it's important, but just so you know we're going to get married as soon as possible so you may have to make another trip up here in a month or two."

"Why the rush? Are you pregnant?" Abby clutched at Jose. "Dear god, I knew she never should have come here."

"Mama, no, but unlike you, I'm not seventeen and I don't want to wait forever. Like you, I don't need a fancy wedding. Love is enough."

Her papi rubbed her mama's back. "Remember when that was enough for us, Abbs?"

"But where will they live? What will they do? Surely they aren't going to stay here?" The Abby that Lilly had grown up with was back. The one that always worried about appearances and keeping up with the trendsetters.

Lilly stiffened, ready for the oncoming argument, but Nate rubbed her back before pulling her closer and taking her hand.

"Mrs. Ramirez, Lilly wants to stay here. There's enough land for her greenhouses. I'll set up my veterinarian practice and she can grow flowers. It'll be a simple life, but that will leave plenty of time for us to be together. That's all we want."

Nate squeezed her hand then kissed the back of her knuckles. "It didn't take long for me to appreciate how strong a woman this daughter of yours is. You did a remarkable job raising her."

"But." She looked from Nate to Jose. "Greenhouses?"

"Maybe you can show me the iris you and grandma developed? I'd love to grow them in my gardens." Lilly followed Nate's lead and stuck with buttering her mother up. It couldn't hurt.

"It's been a long time. I don't know if there are any left, but I can show you where we planted them." Abby sighed in resignation.

"Perfect. Want to join us at church? I can introduce you to my new friends." Lilly quickly changed the subject while she was ahead of the game.

"Is it Catholic?" Jose asked.

"No, but it's very nice, Papi."

"I'll pass on going to the church," he answered.

"Let's talk about this wedding of yours. Where's it going to be?" Abby sat down ready to do some serious planning. It was as if she'd never indulged in a two-and-a-half-week silent treatment, and Lilly was fine letting it go.

"There's this backyard." Lilly blushed and glanced at Nate. They hadn't talked about any of this. "We haven't asked, but since it will just be our families, Eric might let us borrow it."

Nate wrapped his arms around her again. "I think that sounds perfect, as long as there's dancing."

"Nate Pierce, now you're teasing." Lilly laughed.

Her parents exchanged a look and a smile. Jose cleared his throat. "And when do you want to do this?"

"We don't want to wait long. A month, maybe two? It depends on when we can get everyone here. Gael and Nate's sister will be the hardest." Lilly pulled Nate to the larger chair. He sat and she settled in his lap. "We want them both to be here. Gael will need to get leave, and we have to find Natalie."

"What do you mean find?" Jose asked.

Nate turned a few shades of red. "She ran away several years ago, and we haven't found her."

"I'm sorry to hear that." Jose rubbed his chin while Abby rested her hand on his knee.

"It seems no family is without some kind of tragedy these days. What about Nate's parents?" Abby asked. "How do they feel about this?"

"I called them this morning. They'll make it work if it works for all of you."

"This is happening so fast." Abby rubbed her brow. "I don't like it."

"Mama, I know this isn't what you imagined, but all I need is my family with me. Nothing else really matters. Just this man, and all of you."

"But you barely know each other." Abby tried again.

"I know that he accepts me for who I am. He's a good man, a hard worker." Lilly leaned into Nate and took one of his hands in both of hers. "And I love him."

Jose squeezed his wife's hand. "Abbs, why don't we let these two go to church while we make some phone calls. I have some connections that might be able to help us with your sister."

"Really? Thank you, Papi!" Lilly jumped up to hug her father.

Nate stood and shook her father's hand. "Thank you, sir. Any help would be appreciated, and I promise not to take this woman for granted. If you'll give me permission to marry her, I'll do everything in my power to make her happy."

"I know you will. You have my blessing. Now, go on. I've got work to do."

Nate turned to Lilly and laughed. "Sweetheart, why don't you finish your hair while I tell your dad what I know about Natalie's last known plans."

Lilly touched her hair. Half was straight, the other half still had the natural wave in it. Everyone laughed, and she joined them as she imagined what she must look like.

"I'll be ready in five minutes." She stretched up on tiptoes and kissed Nate's cheek.

"I'll wait as long as needed."

EPILOGUE

*T*he weeks flew by. Lilly and Nate worked on throwing together a simple wedding with the help of their new friends while completely turning their lives upside down.

Nate started the process of getting his vet's license registered in Arkansas, and Lilly put together a business plan for her greenhouses. They spent as much time together as possible, but Nate took several trips with Jose to look for his sister. They found her in California.

Lilly wished she could have been with him. She could hear the weariness in his voice when they talked on the phone.

"I can't wait to get home to you," Nate said one night after taking Natalie home to Colorado. "Mom wants me to stay a couple more days, but I need to hold you."

"I miss you too." She wanted to see him, but she knew he needed the time with his family. "How's your sister?"

"She'll be okay. I've never wanted to hurt someone so bad in my life. That no-count boyfriend of hers had her so scared." His voice broke and Lilly hurt with him.

"I'm so sorry. Stay as long as you need to. I'll be here when you're sure your family is safe."

"I love you." He was silent for a moment. "As soon as James gets back from Denver, I'm coming home. The others will come down in two weeks. Think we can be ready by then?"

"I'm ready now." She breathed.

Nate chuckled, making her heart soar. He would be okay. "Can I ask a favor?"

"Anything, Nate."

"Can I pick the song you walk down the aisle to?"

"Why?"

"Because I heard a song today that made me think of you."

"What is it?" she asked.

"It's a surprise."

She could almost hear the smile return to his voice. If it could make him sound happy again, she'd give him anything.

"As long as you're waiting for me, I don't care what plays."

~

*E*ric was happy to loan his yard for the wedding, and although Lilly had tried to keep the guest list small it kept growing. Nate's family, her family, Kerri and her family, Eric, Jen, Jaya, Brynn, Mic, Flo and her husband, Roberta from down the road, the Hanes sisters, the Connors with their many children and grandchildren, and Belinda from Sparky's. Others wanted to come out of curiosity, but Lilly had to draw the line somewhere.

Lilly wore another one of her grandma's dresses. She liked the vintage style and the fit suited her figure. This time she chose one with a white background covered with delicate pink rosettes on green vines. Her mama had only complained once, but then ordered a slip that Selena brought with her from New York to make the dress puff out. Her brothers and sisters were ready to act as bridesmaids and groomsmen, and two of the Connor littles were stepping in as flower girl and ring bearer.

Natalie hadn't wanted to participate, even though they'd asked her. Lilly liked Nate's sister but worried about her. She'd barely spoken to anyone since arriving the day before. Nate told her she'd been stuck in an abusive relationship and it would take a while for her to recover.

Natalie had a strength though. Lilly could see it, and she knew that as soon as Nat learned to trust it again she'd be okay.

The wedding day finally came. By the time Lilly waited to walk down the aisle, she was half crazy to get the whole thing over with. All she wanted was to run away from the circus of visiting family and be alone with Nate.

She stood with her Papi and wondered how she would know when it was time to start. Nate promised her she'd know.

When the music started it wasn't the traditional wedding march. She didn't think it would be, but the song playing from the speakers wasn't anything she could have planned for. All her nerves dissipated and she burst out laughing.

The Latin rhythms of *Despacito* wafted over the yard where she'd first talked about starting a *fuego* with Nate.

Oh, how she loved that man!

"Come on, Papi." She walked around the corner of the house and let the music move her down the aisle.

Stepping and swaying her hips, keeping her gaze focused on Nate. She didn't know what her family did behind her and she didn't care that she'd taken the lead. She danced her way to the man waiting for her.

Nate took her hands when she reached him. "Lilly, I have no rhythm to speak of, but I have every faith you can teach me how to live with the joy you share with everyone around you."

"*Con todo mi corazón.*" She repeated it in English before going on tiptoe to kiss him. "With all my heart."

"That's supposed to come at the end of the ceremony." One of the Hanes sisters called out from the crowd and everyone laughed.

Lilly's heart was full of happiness. She had her family back. Nate had his. And for the first time, she felt like she had a home where she truly fit in.

THANKS FOR READING!

Did you enjoy Landscape Love?
Please take the time to leave a review on Amazon. Sharing
what you liked, and even what you didn't like, is the best way
to help an author.

Leave a review.

ACKNOWLEDGMENTS

Writing is no longer a solitary endeavor. Thank you to all of those people who have encouraged me in one way or another to continue to explore the stories in my imagination. Especially those of my writers group: Tamara, Tammy, and Kirsten. Your weekly insights are making me a better writer.

Thank you to Tamara and Hillary for our frequent trips to Eureka Springs, AR, for lunch dates and innumerable texts and Marco polos discussing our shared characters.

A special thanks to my early readers Patti, Theresa, and Joan, who were willing to give feedback on these stories before I sent it to my editor. Your questions and insights were invaluable!

ABOUT THE AUTHOR

River Ford is the romance pen name of Science Fiction writer Charity Bradford. She's always loved the sweet (and sometimes cheesy) Hallmark movies. One day she decided to give it a try and fell in love with the characters she created to live in Eureka Springs, AR. They were so real, with problems she could understand. It didn't hurt that she could drive to the historic town in an hour and immerse herself in all things Eureka Springs.

EUREKA IN LOVE CHRONOLOGY

Stories do not have to be read in order to be enjoyed.

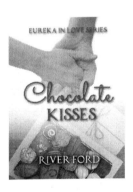

Chocolate Kisses by River Ford (Series Book 1)

Kerri Manning returns home with only one semester of college left. She's in pain and trying to figure out what to do with a diagnosis that will change her future. It's hard to dream of happiness, but the new guy in town manages to make her laugh. Can she take a chance he'll stick around? Eric Hunt is an up and coming sculptor who has grown tired of his fake friends in New York City. He finds himself in the small town of Eureka Springs looking for the passion he used to have for his art. Could Kerri be the inspiration he needs?

Forgetting You by Hillary Ann Sperry (Series Book 2)

Saying it's over, doesn't actually mean that it's over.
Brynn thinks she's finally fought her way out of quiet Eureka Springs and into her destiny. Then, in less than the beat of a breath, tragedy derails her quick and easy getaway. Now she's stuck in the little town she tried so hard to escape. Mic discovered his version of success without having to step outside his own backyard. When Brynn returns home, his life is shaken by things he hasn't felt since she left. It's going to take everything he's got to stay away from the girl who wanted more then he or Eureka Springs could ever offer.

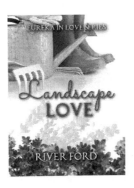

Series Book 3

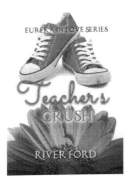

Teacher's Crush by River Ford (Series Book 4 Coming Soon)

Jennifer Carlson has always been the glue that kept her group of friends together, but now that everyone is pairing off she's left jobless. In more ways than one. She's newly graduated and running out of time to secure the coaching position at her alma mater in Eureka Springs. Too bad her first run in with the principal crushes her hopes of getting the job.

Robert Allen doesn't like irresponsible people, and at first glance, the runner taking up his bike trail appears to be the worst kind of offender. However, her sass and attitude make her unforgettable in more pleasurable ways. When she shows up for an interview, Robert has to decide if he wants her to teach, or if he wants her for his very own.

After the Fall by Tamara Hart Heiner (Series Book 5)
Arkansas. Solitude and nature. Time to breathe and rediscover herself. That's what Luce thinks she's getting when she returns home after her divorce. Instead, she meets Connor and falls, once again, in love.

Connor blames his lying and cheating father for his mother's irresponsible behavior, leaving the burden of maintaining the family business squarely on Connor's shoulders. Luce is the unexpected variable that throws off his entire equation, the random x that sends his life into a delicious tilt-a-whirl. She's everything he ever wanted. Minus her divorce.

When Connor's mom falls ill and makes a deathbed request, he knows he'll do his best to oblige her. Even if it means pretending to marry the woman he loves.

Now Available!

88873291R00117

Made in the USA
San Bernardino, CA
18 September 2018